THREESOMES

THE LESBIAN COLLECTION

VICTORIA RUSH

COPYRIGHT

For the uninhibited...

VOLUME ONE

GIRLS' CAMP

1

———

FALLING FOR THE GIRL

I woke to the sound of my phone rattling on the nightstand. I ignored it for a few seconds, then buried my head under my pillow, squeezing the sides trying to muffle the noise. For the last week or so, I'd had more trouble than usual getting my day started. After the girl next door had gone off to college, I felt hopelessly alone and depressed. Even though our affair only lasted a couple of weeks, it had injected an exciting spark into my love life that had been missing for far too long. Now I was all alone again, with only my freelance graphic design job giving me any reason to get out of bed in the morning.

After a few minutes, the phone started buzzing again, and I rolled over to glance at the screen. It was an incoming call from my best friend, Hannah. Normally, she texted me at this time of the day, so it must have been important. I reached over and tapped the speaker button, then flopped back down on the bed.

"Hello?" I said, groggily.

"Are you *still* not up?" Hannah said. "I'm getting worried about you, girl. You haven't set foot out of your place for over two weeks."

"Welcome to the life of a lonely freelance artist. Sometimes I wonder if it was such a good idea quitting the firm. At least you see some familiar faces every day."

"You haven't been answering my texts lately."

"I've been...*busy*."

"Sleeping in and feeling sorry for yourself?"

I paused, thinking how best to respond. I hadn't told Hannah about my recent fling with the girl next door.

"Something like that."

"Listen," she said. "I've been thinking. Summer's almost over. We need to get you out of the house and get your circulation pumping again. Me and some of the girls from the office were thinking of taking a camping trip."

"What, to Yosemite again?"

"Even better. *Canada*. Lilly knows a quiet place way up north that's hardly been touched by human civilization. We can go full-on commando. Portage in by canoe, catch our own fish, go skinny dipping—the whole nine yards. It'll be good for you to get away for a while. Just you and me and four other girls."

The idea of swimming in the nude with people I knew made me feel a bit uncomfortable. I still hadn't come out with Hannah or anyone else about my recent lesbian dalliances.

"Skinny dipping? Won't it be *cold* up there? That doesn't sound like my idea of relaxing."

"The lakes are small and shallow, not like Lake Michigan. They get super-warm this time of the year. Plus, they're crystal clear and utterly pristine. Lilly says you can actually *drink* from them. When was the last time you felt comfortable doing that?"

I glanced out my window toward Abby's house and sighed.

"I don't know, Han..."

"Well I'm not letting you off the hook this time," Hannah said. "We've already booked the tickets. We fly into Toronto Wednesday morning, drive a rental car north for a few hours, then arrive back home middle of next week. Your freelance business can survive without your attention for a week."

"What—no laptops? Do they have cell reception up there?"

"No, and no. The only thing you're allowed to pack that has any kind of battery is your vibrator. But we'll be too busy having other kinds of fun to think about sex. Building campfires, roasting marshmallows, running away from bears—"

"Bears?"

"Just kidding. They do have black bears in that neck of the woods, but Lilly says as long as we keep a clean campsite, they'll leave us alone. Are you in?"

I rolled over and pulled my duvet over my shoulders.

"Arghh. I suppose so. As long as I can bring my comforter with me."

"No way," Hannah said. "We have to pack light, just the necessities. We're going to be carrying everything in and out on our back, including the canoes. Three tents, some air mattresses, sleeping bags, and a minimum of provisions. We'll catch everything else we need."

"Fine. As long as I don't have to clean the fish."

Hannah chuckled.

"Lilly's our designated cook. She grew up not far from where we're going. She'll show us how to catch, clean, and cook everything."

Hannah paused for a moment over the line.

"Are you going to be able to drag yourself out of bed at five a.m. this Wednesday to catch the early flight?"

"Go away!" I said, pulling the comforter over my head. "I'll call you later today to finalize the arrangements."

"Atta girl. You're gonna love this. The sky is so clear at night, it practically looks like cream, there are so many stars. It'll be just us girls and the cry of the loon over the still water."

"And bears. Don't forget about the bears."

Early Wednesday morning, Hannah picked me up at my place and we drove to O'Hare airport together. She was excited about the trip, but I was still having second thoughts about going away with so many people I knew. No one yet knew about my recent lesbian experiences—not even Hannah—and I wasn't sure if I'd be able to hide my attraction to six scantily-clad women alone in the wilderness.

"You've been awfully quiet lately," she said, glancing at me watching the cars go by.

"I've just been doing a lot of thinking lately. You know, after the divorce, it's been a little...strange. Not knowing what to do with myself, not having anybody to share intimate moments with..."

"Well nothing's going to happen staying holed up alone in your house, that's for sure. You've got to get back on the horse. I've been trying to take you out to the bar for quite a while now—"

I shook my head and sighed.

"That's just not my scene anymore, Han. I'm getting too...*old* for those pick-up routines."

Hannah took her eyes off the road for a moment and stared at me.

"But you still like *men*, right? I hope you haven't lost your mojo. You're just reaching your sexual prime—"

"It's still there. I guess I'm just looking for the...right one."

"Well let's not worry about any of that for a few days. It's just going to be us girls in the middle of nowhere, with no one around for miles. We don't need no stinking men where we're going!"

I huffed an awkward chuckle, then looked out my window at the passing traffic.

The drive north from Toronto into the Canadian interior was stunning. I marveled at all the pretty rivers and lakes alongside the highway, dotted with pretty boathouses and motor yachts plying the dark blue water. The landscape got increasingly rugged the further we got from the city, and about halfway to our final destination we stopped at an outfitter's to rent two canoes. We chose the top-of-the-line skiffs made of fiberglass and kevlar, and I was surprised how easy it was to lift them up and strap them to the top of our big SUV.

Lilly sat up front while Hannah provided navigation using a crumpled old map from her childhood. Bonnie and Madison, who I already knew from my previous job, sat in the middle seat, while I sat in the rear jumper seat with the new girl, Emma. It was hard keeping my attention focused on the passing scenery with her downy legs poking through skimpy cargo shorts rubbing against me on the cramped bench.

She was a little younger than the rest of us, somewhere in her late twenties I estimated, but absolutely gorgeous. Long corkscrew-curly hair tumbled over her plump youthful cheeks and pretty rosebud lips. She reminded me of the college girl Abby, and I kept stealing glances at her exposed legs whenever she peered out her window.

"Everything okay back there?" Hannah called from the front seat, peering into the rearview mirror. "Jade, are you and Emma getting caught up? You're the only ones who don't really know each other. I hope you guys are making friends—we've got a long trip ahead of us."

"Emma's a doll," I said, stealing another quick glance at her. "We've been pointing out our favorite boathouses along the way. This really is God's country up here."

"You haven't seen anything yet," Lilly said, from the front seat. "What 'til you get to Algonquin Park. It's even *more* beautiful up there. No boats, no cars, and no people. Just the quietest, most serene lake country you'll ever experience."

"How did you know about this place?" Madison chimed in from the middle seat.

"My grandparents had a cottage on Lake Muskoka, not too far from here. I used to spend every summer there growing up, water-skiing during the day, lying on the dock to get a tan, entertaining friends at night. My granddad was the one who taught me how to fish. There's nothing like the taste of fresh-caught smallmouth bass cooked in a skillet with nothing but butter. You guys are going to die and thought you'd gone to heaven."

"If I don't die first watching you cut its head off," I joked.

The last few miles to our embarkation point took us along a narrow gravel road through thick maple and birch trees. We could hear the overhanging branches scraping against the hulls of the overturned canoes on the roof of our car, and I smiled at Emma when she reached over and grasped my hand in excitement. The road terminated in a thicket by a small parking lot, and we locked our car near a beat-up old Pathfinder, then lifted our heavy backpacks loaded with provisions onto our shoulders.

Lilly and Hannah took the lead carrying the first canoe, while Bonnie and Madison followed close behind carrying the second one. Emma and I took up the rear, keeping a nervous watch out for bears. The trail was narrow and rough, with plenty of dips and boulders to navigate. I was glad I'd brought my hiking shoes as I stepped gingerly over the slippery moss-covered rocks.

"Are we there yet?" I called ahead to Hannah and Lilly, only half-kidding.

"It's about thirty more minutes to the main lake where we'll put in," Lilly said. "But there's a pretty waterfall about halfway where we can rest and freshen up."

"Suck it up, trooper," Hannah said. "Don't be a pussy. We haven't even got to the hard part yet. Enjoy the scenery. Can't you smell the fresh scent of the Great White North?"

"I thought that was the scent of your stinky armpits," I joked.

Fifteen minutes later, we began to hear the distant sound of a waterfall as the trail began to get steeper and more treacherous. The girls carrying the canoes had to walk carefully so as not to lose their footing and topple the canoes from their shoulders. I suddenly felt guilty about not carrying my weight.

"Do you guys need a third?" I shouted ahead. "Those canoes look pretty heavy. I'm happy to lend another shoulder."

"It's actually easier to maneuver with two than three," Lilly said. "But after our rest stop, I'll be happy to switch if you're still game. It's getting a bit hot under here. I could use some fresh air."

The sound of falling water grew louder and louder until we came upon a small, sloped waterfall at the side of our trail.

"Let's stop here and cool off for a bit," Lilly said. "Do you guys feel like a refreshing shower?"

"Hell, yes!" Hannah said, as she and Lilly lifted the canoe off their shoulders and lowered it to the ground.

I looked at everybody's cargo pants, fleece vests, and heavy hiking boots.

"Aren't we a little overdressed?" I said.

"It's just us girls out here," Hannah replied, beginning to strip off her outerwear. "Who needs clothes?"

She and Lilly stripped down to their bra and panties, then they paused and looked at the rest of us playfully.

"Fuck it," Hannah said. "There's no one around. Let's go au naturel."

The two girls unclasped their bras then pulled their panties off and scampered into the waterfall, laughing as the water splashed against their bare chest and asses.

"What are you guys waiting for?" Hannah said, looking at the rest of us hesitating on the bank of the waterfall. "It's warm, clean, and refreshing. Strip off your clothes and join us!"

The four of us glanced at one another for a few seconds, then we quickly disrobed and joined Hannah and Lilly in the waterfall. At first it was a bit of a shock feeling the cool water on my hot skin, but it didn't take long to get used to it. After a few minutes, it felt just like a warm shower.

I'd barely had a chance to glimpse at the naked bodies of the other girls before they scrambled into the waterfall, but with the running water tumbling over us, it was a feast to take in. We were all in good shape from regular yoga and gym classes, but there was something about Emma's figure that I couldn't take my eyes off. She had a more slender, youthful figure, and I stole glances at her pointed nipples on her perky breasts as the water cascading over her tight chest and abdomen. Her bare pussy shined in the sunlight as the liquid fingers teased and danced over her glistening mound.

"What'd I tell you?" Hannah said, blinking at me as the water crashed over her head. "Isn't it glorious? Warm, refreshing, and *unspoiled.*"

Lilly tipped her head as she opened her mouth wide under the falling water.

"Feel free to rehydrate," she gurgled. "This is the cleanest water you'll find just about anywhere on earth. Lop it up!"

We all tilted our heads back and giggled and spat at one another as we stretched our arms out, feeling the warm current passing over us. After a few minutes, Lilly began tiptoeing over the steep rocks lining the waterfall toward the other side of the cataract.

"Come on, you guys," she said. "There's something else I want to show you. Just be careful as you step on these slippery rocks. I don't want anybody falling down the waterfall."

"Um, *yeah*," I said, glancing down the steep embankment to the bottom of the waterfall thirty feet below.

We followed Lilly through the falling water, grasping onto the sides of exposed outcroppings to make sure we had a firm handhold and stepping carefully onto the rocks to be sure we had a solid footing. When we all got to the other side, she giggled and ran off into the bush. We had no idea where she was going, but after about twenty feet through the thick brush, we stopped at the top of a sheer cliff overlooking a lake thirty feet below.

We stood there for a moment trying not to gape at each other's wet naked bodies, then peered at Lilly warily.

"What do you say?" she said. "Are you guys game?"

"What?!" Madison exclaimed. "You mean *jump*? Off *this*? Down *there*?"

"Are you *crazy*?" Bonnie said. "We'll *kill* ourselves!'

"It's only thirty feet or so," Lilly said. "I've done it plenty of times. It doesn't even hurt. Just be sure to put your hands over your peachka and keep your legs together so you don't get too much of a slap between your legs. Last one in is a pussy!"

Lilly screeched as she jumped off the cliff while we peered over the ledge and watched her splash into the still water below. Five seconds later, she emerged from under the surface and screamed with delight as she motioned for us to follow.

We all looked at one another with wide eyes, then Hannah, Bonnie, and Madison followed soon after. I glanced at Emma with a mix of trepidation and lust. Part of my hesitation was not wanting to be the last one following the girls into the pool below, but the other part of me just wanted to stay on top and take in Emma's sweet nubile body as long as I could. She kept her body shyly turned away from me so I couldn't see her bare mound while she quivered holding her arms tightly across her chest. The other girls were taunting us from below and I knew that sooner or later one of us would have to go.

"Are you up for this?" I said, watching her quaking in fear.

"I dunno," Emma said. "It's a long way down."

"How about if we hold hands and do it together?" I said.

Emma looked at me uncertainly for a moment, then nodded and edged closer to me. Then she held out her hand and I clasped it gently. I could feel her hand shaking, and I squeezed it to build her confidence.

"On the count of three, okay?" I said.

Emma nodded as I began the count.

"One...two...*three!*" I yelled as Emma and I leaped off the cliff together into the bracing water below.

That wasn't the only leap that Emma and I would take over the next few days.

2
______

NIGHT WHISPERS

We swam for a few minutes in the warm water of the lake below the waterfall, then retrieved our gear and completed our portage down to the shore. The experience of paddling the canoes across the quiet lake was sublime. There was virtually no noise other than the occasional cry of a bird and the soft sloshing sound of our paddles dipping in and out of the water. Little black bugs skittered over the surface as the bows of our canoes sliced through the shimmering liquid. Every now and then I'd hear a droplet sound near our boat followed by little concentric ripples in the water.

"What's that sound?" I asked Lilly, who'd taken up the stern position in my canoe. "It sounds like someone throwing pebbles in the water."

"It's fish feasting on all those water skeeters," she said. "They're a pretty tempting snack just sitting there on the surface."

"What *kind* of fish?" Hannah asked, peering over the gunwale into the dark water from her squatted position in the middle of our canoe. "Should we be worried about us being fish food for some kind of monster dwelling under the surface? It's pretty dark down there. I can barely see two feet below the surface."

Lilly chuckled as she dragged her paddle in the water to steer our canoe gently to the starboard side.

"The water's actually remarkably clear when you're underneath it. But you needn't worry about any Jaws-like predator under the surface. It's mostly filled with Walleye, Pike, Bass, and Yellow Perch. Though some of the Muskies do grow to five or six feet in length, they only have teeth big enough to eat smaller fish."

Hannah peered over to the other canoe knifing through the water a few feet away.

"What about *Emma*?" she said, smiling at the cute girl next to us. "By those standards, I'd say she qualifies as 'smaller fish'. You better watch out you don't get gobbled up by one of those things, Emma!"

Emma turned her head in Hannah's direction and peered over her sunglasses, then continued quietly paddling the front of her canoe. I watched her toned arms rippling and her little breasts shaking on her chest as her ass wiggled on her seat from the paddling motion.

"Where's a good place to set up camp?" I asked Lilly.

She looked around the lake and saw a small rocky outcropping about half a mile to our northeast.

"There's an island over that way," she said pointing to the peninsula. "We should have it all to ourselves, and if I remember correctly, there's a quiet little bay behind it that should make for perfect bass fishing. We can all give it a try later and see if we can catch something fresh for dinner."

"When you say all to *ourselves*, do you mean no bears?" I asked.

Lilly chuckled at my first-time camping trepidation.

"I meant in terms of other campers. We probably won't run into anybody else this far from civilization, but I did notice another car in the parking lot at our trailhead. As for bears, they're pretty good swimmers, but as long as we keep our food locked up and sealed, they should leave us alone."

"I'm not sure I'm comfortable with the *should* part of that statement," I said.

W hen we got to the island, we found a small beach and pulled our canoes ashore. We unpacked the boats and located a flat mossy section in the center of the island to pitch our three tents. There were six girls, with each tent comfortably accommodating two air mattresses and two sleeping bags. We contemplated drawing straws to see who would sleep with whom, then we all just giggled and threw our gear in whichever tent was closest. Hannah joined me, Maddie and Lilly took the next, and Emma and Bonnie took the last. I peered over at Emma's tent as she got down on her knees and wiggled her ass through the front canopy, suddenly wishing I'd joined her.

After we set up camp, we set out in pairs to collect kindling and driftwood for a fire, then we had a refreshing swim in our bikinis to cool off. I was surprised how hot it got by mid-afternoon, and the water, though still warm, provided a handy respite from the heat. Soon after, Lilly collected the fishing rods and tackle, and we all walked over to the far end of the island overlooking a small bay filled with water lilies.

"Now I see why you like to come here," Hannah chuckled, scanning the idyllic scene. "It's filled with your favorite type of flowers."

"Yeah, well those lilies also provide perfect cover for bass and perch. We've got our own little seafood restaurant hiding under those pretty flowers."

She reached down onto the ground and picked up a fishing rod.

"Who knows how to use these things?"

We all just looked at her dumbfounded.

"No worries," she said. "Let me show you how it's done."

She connected the loose pieces of the shaft then attached a red and white striped metal lure to the end of the fishing line. Then she stepped about ten feet back from our group and looked out over the shore.

"Okay," she said. "The most important thing is that you don't snare yourself or anyone else as you're casting your line into the water. Which is why you'll need to separate yourself from your next nearest fisherwoman by at least ten to fifteen feet."

"Fisherwoman?" I teased. "Is that what your grandpappy used to call you?"

"Not exactly. But hey, there's no guys out here, so I'm improvising. Fisherperson, fisherman, angler, whatever. Now listen up. After I get your rods and lures assembled, you hold the rod like this."

Lilly held the rod out firmly in front of her, gripping the cork handle.

"Like you're giving it a firm handshake, with your middle and forefingers threaded under the handle of the reel."

"Or like you're giving it a firm hand job," Hannah snickered.

"Now..." Lilly continued, rolling her eyes. "Hold the rod out beside you and make sure you've got about two feet of line hanging down from the tip of the rod, like this."

"Like a horny cock dripper..." Hannah said, continuing the metaphor.

"Behave, Hannah," Lilly admonished her friend, "or I'm gonna slap your ass. Now, press and hold this little release button on your reel, then turn your body sideways, holding the rod out in front of you. Then swing your arm quickly out in the direction you want your lure to land and release the button just before you get to the end, like this."

Lilly deftly swung the rod with her wrist and we watched her lure sail about forty feet over the water and plop just short of a bunch of water lilies.

"I'm attaching bobbers to the ends of your lines so you shouldn't have to worry about your line getting caught on rocks underwater."

"*Bobbers*? *Rods*? *Swinging*?" Hannah joked. "You gotta admit it sounds a bit like—"

"Put your dick in your pants, Hannah," Lilly said. "Try to concentrate, will you, so we all don't starve out here?

"When you cast your lure," she continued, "try not to get too close to the flowers or your line will get caught up there too. You may need to practice a few times to get the hang of it, but after a few swings, you should be casting like a champ. After your lure lands in the water, start turning the crank on the reel counterclockwise slowly so your lure will swim through the water looking like a real fish."

"What if we *catch* something?" Bonnie asked.

"You'll feel a tug on your line and some sudden tension in your reel. Just steady your rod and crank the fish in slowly toward shore. Give me a shout if you need any help. Once your fish gets close to shore, I'll use my net to land him. Then I'll tie him up to this little stringer to keep him fresh underwater until we eat."

"Until you chop off his head and gut and cook him, you mean," Hannah joked.

Emma hunched her shoulders and winced.

"Poor little fishes," she said. "They'll just be going about minding their own business when suddenly a hook tears into their flesh. Then we'll yank them by their mouth out of their element and tie them up while they wait to be guillotined. How barbaric!"

"Hey, it's a fish-eat-fish world out there, Emms," Lilly chuckled. "We just happen to be the biggest fish at the top of the food chain. If I remember correctly, we don't have any vegetarians among us, do we?"

Lilly paused for a moment to make sure everybody was on board.

"Right, let's get started then. If anybody wants to sit this one out and just watch the rest of us, that's cool. If we're feeling generous, we might share some of our catch with you later."

Lilly proceeded to assemble each of our rods, then we separated along the bank and awkwardly practiced casting into the bay. It didn't take me too long to get the hang of it, and after five or six casts I was able to fling my lure almost as far as Lilly with similar accuracy. I glanced over at Emma standing fifteen feet to my right and noticed her huffing and cursing as her lure jerked and plopped into the water only a few feet in front of her.

I stepped behind her and reached around, grasping her rod with my two hands.

"Hey, Emma," I said. "Let me see if I can help you. The key is in timing the button release at the right moment."

I positioned Emma's thumb over the button on the reel, then placed my thumb over hers. Then I pulled the rod gently behind us a few feet and swung her arms forward in a sudden jerk.

"*Release!*" I yelled as we watched her lure go sailing twenty feet into the bay.

"Yayyyy!" Emma squealed with delight.

Then she turned around and kissed me on the cheek.

"Thanks, Jade. You're an awesome fisherwoman. Don't go too far away. I still might need you to show me how to wiggle my hips properly to make this work."

I looked into Emma's eyes and smiled as I felt my cheeks warm with a gentle flush.

"You got it, girl," I said. "I'll keep one eye on you from my perch right over there."

Truth was, I kept more than one eye on her wiggling ass in her tight bikini as she continued casting her rod. After about ten minutes of quiet casting into the still waters of the bay, Emma suddenly began hyperventilating.

"I think I've got something!" she squealed, as we watched the tip of her rod twitch and bend in frenetic tugs.

"Okay, Emm," Lilly said, rushing over. "Just hold your rod steady and slowly crank the handle of your reel away from you. There's no rush—let him tucker himself out for a bit before you try to outmuscle him."

She looked at the deep bend in Lilly's rod and nodded.

"It looks like a big one, maybe a five-pounder. That might be enough to feed all of us tonight. Be cool, girl—take your time. Just remember, you're stronger than he is."

We all cheered Emma on as she struggled to control her fluttering rod and awkwardly reel in the fish. When it got close to shore, it jumped two feet out of the water and waved twice rapidly in the air before diving back under the surface.

Lilly stepped down onto the bank with a fishnet and stepped into the water as the fish neared shore, then swung the net underwater and lifted it up for us to see. As the bass flapped wildly in the tangled rope, Lilly calmly reached down and removed the hook from its mouth. Then she threaded her fingers under its gills and held the fish up for everybody to see.

"Woo-hoo!" Emma yelped, proud that she'd caught the first fish of the day.

"Good job, Emm," Hannah said, and we all clapped and smiled to acknowledge her accomplishment.

Lilly attached Emma's catch to the stringer chain underwater, then the group fished for another thirty minutes until we'd caught three more bass.

"That should do it if you guys want to take a breather," Lilly said, placing the stringer of fish in a metal pail filled with water. "Time to cook these fellas up and see what real Canadian food tastes like."

The sun was beginning to lower on the horizon, and after taking another short swim to cool off, we all got dressed in cargo pants and polar fleeces to protect ourselves against the mosquitos and evening chill. I watched Lilly deftly cut off the head of each fish then expertly fillet the flesh to remove it from the thin skeleton underneath.

"Looks like you've done this before," I said, marveling at her skill.

"A few hundred times maybe," she said.

I stood mesmerized as she sliced the fish under its belly and removed its entrails, then carefully pulled the flanks away from the spiny skeleton inside.

"Kind of messy, huh?"

"Yeah, it's a bit gross at first, but you get used to it pretty quick. My mouth is already watering thinking about the taste."

While Lilly filleted the fish, the other girls collected some small logs and rocks from around the shore and placed them in concentric circles in the middle of our campsite to build a fire pit. Then they placed some twigs and driftwood inside the rocky pit and started a small fire. After it quieted down a bit, Lilly placed a steel grate and a cast iron pan over the hole and slapped a few slivers of butter in the pan along with the fillets. Before long, the aroma of fresh pan-seared fish wafted into the air.

"That smells exquisite, Lilly," Hannah said, suddenly emerging from her tent. "Do you need us to help prepare any sides?"

Lilly shook her head.

"For our first night together, I just want you to savor this, straight-up. All we need to finish it off is some lemon slices cut up and some paper plates and forks."

When the fish was done, we all sat around the campfire on the wooden logs while Lilly served us our plates.

"*Oh my God,* Lilly," Bonnie said, placing the first morsel in her mouth, closing her eyes and tilting her head back. "This is to *die* for! Now I don't feel nearly as bad about yanking those little critters out of their cozy lily garden."

"What about *you*, Emma?" Lilly said, glancing in her direction. "Are you comfortable with eating your catch?"

"Um, *yeah*," Emma said, as she gobbled the fish down.

"Mmmm," Hannah chimed in. "What *is* it exactly that makes this so good? This tastes even better than at the top-rated seafood restaurant in the city."

"Who knows?" Emma said, shaking her head. "It could just be because we're eating it truly fresh-caught. Maybe it's the lemon and butter seasoning."

"Or maybe it's just that pristine freshwater Canadian goodness coming through," I joked.

After we finished eating, Lilly placed the entrails and fish heads back in the water, then we washed our cutlery and bagged up our plates and hung our trash from a rope over a high tree branch to keep the bears away. As dusk set in, we built our fire back up and huddled around the pit in a circle.

"What now?" Hannah said. "What do six girls do for fun after dark on a lonely island in the middle of nowhere? Tell spooky stories?"

"*Stories* could be fun," Maddie said. "But they don't have to be spooky. I'm already creeped out enough about the idea of sleeping in that flimsy tent with so many bears within swimming distance. How about some *fun* stories?"

"I know!" Bonnie said. "Let play *Truth or Dare*. That outta get our juices going. Who wants to go first?"

"Truth, or *dare*?" Hannah asked.

"Truth," Bonnie said. "Tell us something daring about yourself that none of us know."

"Hmmm," Hannah said, looking up trying to think of some sordid detail from her past that she was willing to share. "Well—I once spent a night in jail."

"No way!" Emma said, her eyes widening in disbelief.

"*Way*," Hannah said. "Though granted it was only for a couple of hours. I was sixteen and got caught for shoplifting. I think the sheriff in my small town wanted to make an example of me to scare the shit out of me."

"Did it work?" Lilly asked.

"I wasn't really scared, because I was all alone in my cell and I kind of knew what they were trying to do. I was more scared about what my father was going to do to me when he bailed me out."

"And?" I said.

"Grounded for three months. Which is like three *years* when you're sixteen. So yeah, I guess it worked insofar as discouraging me from doing something like that again."

"What did you steal?" Bonnie asked.

"A vibrator from the local sex shop. I was too embarrassed to actually buy it, so I tried to sneak it out under my coat instead."

"That'll teach you to play with naughty things before your time," Lilly winked at Hannah.

"What about *you*, Lil?" Hannah said. "What naughty things have you done that we don't know about?"

"*Welll*," Lilly said, stretching out the word for dramatic effect. "I engaged in some technically illegal sex not too long ago...."

"Mmmm, *yummy*," Hannah said. "Do tell. There's not many things that are illegal anymore in that area."

"It was an underage boy. *Sixteen* to be exact. The captain of my son's football team. We were at the boy's parents' house celebrating their championship and he and I were alone having a chat, and one thing led to another. We slipped into the ravine behind his yard and had a quickie."

"A *quickie*?" Hannah teased. "That hardly sounds like fun. Was he nicely hung at least?"

"He definitely came equipped with a decent package. But you know boys at that age. They can't last very long—"

"What exactly did you two do?" I probed for more details.

"I just gave him a quick blowjob. I was too terrified we'd be found out. But it was fun and definitely satisfying."

"For at least *one* of you!" Madison said.

"I suppose," Lilly said. "How about you, Maddie? What kinky things have you gotten into that we don't know about?"

Maddie paused for a moment trying to conjure up a sufficiently juicy story.

"Well, my husband and I just had anal sex for the first time last week—"

"Which *one*?" Hannah said. "You or *him*?"

"*Hannah!*" Bonnie scolded, shooting Hannah a disapproving look. "That's prying a little too deep. Let Maddie tell the story."

"What?" Hannah said. "I'm just saying, she could have used a strap-on, or something. Some guys are into that sort of thing—"

"It was *me*, if you must know," Maddie said. "I mean *receiving*, that is."

"What's that like?" Emma said, scrunching up her nose in disgust. "I mean, doesn't it hurt?"

"Oooh," Hannah teased. "I guess we know at least *one* of us has never tried this. Poor little Emma, leading such a sheltered life..."

Emma lowered her head and frowned as she peered into the fire. I wanted to walk over to her log and put my arms around her. It was cruel of Hannah to put her on the spot like that and make her feel small.

"Well it didn't hurt exactly," Maddie continued. "But I wouldn't say

I enjoyed it as much as the usual way. My husband certainly did though, judging by his moans of delight."

Everybody paused for a moment as the girls looked at me and Emma to see who would go next. Hannah glanced over at Emma still sulking on her log and finally broke the silence.

"What about you, Jade? What kind of fun adventures have you been up to lately? I mean besides sleeping in and working on your graphic design projects?"

I looked at Hannah with a sly smile. If she *only* knew. I probably had accumulated enough kinky stories just in the last couple of months to outdo everybody around the campfire. But I still wasn't ready to share my most personal secret.

"Well, I recently had a little remote affair with one of my neighbors..." I started.

"*Remote*?" Hannah said. "As in not face-to-face? Was it telephone sex or webcam sex?"

"Neither. We just watched each other through our windows at night. It was actually pretty hot."

"Oh? Is this someone you've had your eye on for a while? Is he hot? What did you guys do?"

"Yes, I've had my eye on him for a while now," I lied, not wanting to tell the girls that it was actually Abby, the college girl next door. "We've been watching each other around our adjoining pools for some time. But he's married, so I never felt comfortable making the first move."

"So, what did he do? Flash you from his private study while his wife was doing the dishes?"

"I think his wife was away for a few days. It was late at night, and I caught him coming out of the shower with his bedroom light on. I guess he caught me watching him and one thing led to another..."

"So you both rubbed one out watching each other?"

"Yeah. But it was just a one-time thing. His wife came home the next day and I didn't want to take any more chances at getting caught."

"Well that definitely qualifies as semi-hot," Lilly said.

Everybody turned to Emma, who glanced nervously out of the corner of her eyes at the rest of the group.

"That just leaves you, Em," Lilly said. "What sordid details have you been holding back about yourself?"

Emma paused for a long moment as she glanced at her friends around the campfire.

"Well, I once did it with a...*girl*. You know, at college."

My panties instantly moistened as I squirmed uncomfortably on my log.

"It was with my roommate. We were both pretty drunk after a party, so I'm not even sure it qualifies—"

"Oh, I think it *definitely* qualifies," Hannah said. "You've got to give us at least a few details. What did you two do exactly?"

"You know, the usual stuff. There's only so many things two girls can do together, right?"

"*Boo!*" Hannah jeered. "Not good enough. You've got to give us at least one detail."

"Well," Emma hesitated. "It started with us both lamenting how neither of us had hooked up in a long time. One thing led to another, and we ended up making out on my bed."

The more I listened to Emma, the more I could feel a large wet spot spreading in my cargo pants between my legs. I shimmied toward a knot on my log and quietly rubbed my clit against the stump in the dark as Emma told her story.

"*Making out?*" Hannah said. "What do you mean? Kissed, fondled, sucked, scissored—we want details!"

I could see Emma shifting nervously on her log, beginning to feel uncomfortable about sharing any more details.

"You know," I interrupted. This whole time we've been telling truths and we haven't even had a single dare. I've got a dare for everybody. I dare you all to strip off your clothes and go skinny dipping in the lake with the big old muskies and snapping turtles!"

"If we don't get eaten alive by the *mosquitoes* first!" Bonnie protested.

"Not if we get in the water fast enough," I said, stripping off my clothes. "Last one in a rotten egg!" I scampered over the pine needles of our campsite and ran into the water at our little beach.

"Come on in, you scaredy-cats!" I taunted from the water. "The water's warmer than the air. It's like taking a bath."

The rest of the girls quickly disrobed and scurried into the water, where we splashed and spit water at each other's faces and playfully dove under the surface groping each other. After about ten minutes, we all scampered out of the water and toweled dry, then rushed into our tents and zipped up the flaps to keep the mosquitoes out.

I scolded Hannah for putting Emma on the spot earlier, then we talked a little bit about work before falling asleep early from all the sun and fresh air. But about thirty minutes later, I woke to the sound of rustling not far from our tent. Thinking it might be a bear foraging through our camp, I was about to wake Hannah when I heard the unmistakable sound of a woman moaning. I lay perfectly still and held my breath straining to listen.

The sound was coming from the direction of Bonnie and Emma's tent. I lifted the privacy flap up over the mosquito net window on my side of the tent and peered into the darkness. They'd left a small flashlight on inside their tent, and I could see the shadows of two figures lying next to one another, rubbing their bodies together.

They're making out! I thought.

Suddenly, I wished I'd tried harder to pair up with Emma in her tent. I was envious of Bonnie having her all to herself. Obviously, Emma's story had gotten more than just *me* worked up, and after they'd returned to their tent stark naked, one thing had led to another.

Fuck! I whispered out loud, thrusting my hand under my sleeping bag, beginning to circle my clit.

As I strained to catch whatever I could pick up from the tent next door, I began to hear gasps and moans radiating into the still night. I couldn't make out if it was Emma's or Bonnie's voice, or both of them. But it didn't matter. I was insanely turned on just listening to them, trying to imagine what the two of them were doing.

I squinted through the mosquito netting trying to discern their movement, but I just saw a jumbled clump of shadows shifting in the soft backlight. Suddenly, one of the figures rolled on top of the other, and I saw the unmistakable shape of a naked ass raising and lowering onto the person beneath.

Oh my God. Now they're humping each other!

I wanted to dash out of my tent and join the girls in their fun and feel Emma's sweet pussy between my own legs. *Oh—how much pleasure I could give her,* I thought. I sped up the movement of my fingers over my clit, trying to control my breathing and movement so as not to wake Hannah.

Suddenly, the figure on top raised up to a kneeling position and the girl on the bottom pulled her legs up into a bent knee position. Then the girl on top squatted over her and lowered herself onto her partner below. When the girl on top began shimmying her hips, I saw her full breasts swaying in the backlight and realized for the first time that Emma was on the bottom.

Emma doesn't have tits that full and round, I thought. *Bonnie's full-on fucking her!*

I could hear the women's breathing becoming louder and more ragged, building toward a climax. I jammed two fingers into my cunt and began thrusting as hard as I dared without waking Hannah from the squeaking of my air mattress shifting on the soft ground below us.

Suddenly, the moans escalated in urgency, as Emma thrashed her head from side to side in the throes of pleasure.

"Yes, Bonnie!" I heard her whisper. "Fuck me harder. I'm going to come!"

My pussy suddenly clamped down on my fingers as my orgasm washed over me, and I bit my lip trying to stifle my moans.

"I'm coming, Bonnie!" Emma whispered. "Come with me! Fuuuck —I'm coming!"

Bonnie sped up the humping motion of her hips against Emma, then she suddenly stopped as I saw her chest and torso jerking spastically in the soft backlight.

"Uhnnn," she grunted, as she came inside Emma's sweet tight pussy. "Fuck, yes," she said. "I'm coming, baby!"

I twitched and spasmed inside my sleeping bag as I came along with the two girls, trying desperately not to awaken Hannah sleeping mere inches beside me. When Bonnie finally collapsed on top of Emma and their light switched off, I rubbed out two more orgasms before falling blissfully asleep with the warm stickiness between my legs.

3

BEST FRIENDS

I woke to the cry of a loon echoing over the still lake. Hannah was still sleeping, so I put on some warm clothes and quietly unzipped the front of our tent. Lilly and Madison were huddled around the fire pit with some mugs in their hands and I joined them.

"Morning, Jade," Lilly said. "Did you sleep well?"

"Like a baby. It must be all this fresh air and clean living. Hannah and I fell fast asleep shortly after our swim last night."

"No bear nightmares or intrusions?" Lilly chuckled.

"No, thank God," I said, wondering if Lilly and Maddie had heard the noise from Bonnie and Emma's tent. "Though I *did* hear some other rustling around the camp..."

"Oh?" Lilly said. "It might have been raccoons trying to steal our leftovers."

She looked up at the high tree branch where our garbage bag from last night still dangled twenty feet off the ground.

"Looks like they weren't able to solve our little challenge."

She handed me a steaming mug filled with dark fluid.

"Would you like some hot chocolate? Sorry we don't have fresh coffee, but we couldn't exactly fit a coffee maker in our backpacks."

I nodded at Lilly and took the mug between my two hands to warm my fingers.

"We're really roughing it, eh?" I said.

"Good one!" Lilly smiled at me. "You see—you're already starting to sound like a real Canadian."

I peered out across the quiet lake and marveled at the serene beauty of the landscape. The water was smooth as glass, and the sunrise reflected over the surface in a dimpled crimson glow. Tall evergreen trees rose from the rocky shore surrounding the lake, and there was no sign of movement other than a pair of low-flying geese skimming low over the water.

"It's gorgeous out here. You were right, Lilly. It's just as magnificent as you said it would be."

I took a sip of my hot chocolate, then peered up at her.

"So, what's on the agenda today? More skinny dipping and fish-wrangling?"

Lilly chuckled.

"We'll wait 'til the rest of the girls get up. But I was thinking maybe another canoe ride and some more exploring. There's so much natural beauty to explore up here. We can try trolling for fish in the deep water. Maybe we'll catch a pike or a muskie. That'd be enough to feed us for a whole week!"

I heard the sound of a zipper opening as Hannah stepped out of our tent groggily.

"Morning, sleepy-head!" I called out. "Who's the lazy morning person *now*?"

"Ha!" Hannah said, taking a seat beside me on the log. "We're supposed to be chilling up here, remember? I haven't slept this well in a long time."

"So you didn't hear our little visitor last night?" I asked, probing to see if she'd been woken up by Bonnie and Emma's little play date.

"We had a *visitor*?"

"I just heard a bit of rustling around the camp." I glanced up toward our hanging trash bag. "Lilly thinks it might have been a raccoon trying to reach our little waste receptacle."

"Speaking of," Hannah said. "I think I need to do a little disposal of my own. What's the protocol up here?"

Lilly reached behind her log and threw Hannah a roll of toilet paper.

"Do as the bears do," she said. "There's a small spade over by the tree. If you can dig a shallow hole and bury it when you're done, it'll help keep the place clean for other campers."

"Man—" Hannah huffed, "we really *are* roughing it, aren't we?"

Shortly after Hannah trudged off into the brush behind us, Emma and Bonnie emerged from their tent. I was glad that no one other than me had apparently heard them frolicking last night, as they approached our group tentatively. I poured some hot water from the steaming pot on the fire into two empty mugs, then emptied two packets of hot chocolate mix into the water and stirred it with a small stick.

"Hey, you two," I said, handing them each a mug. "Welcome to the party. Did you sleep well?"

Emma took a seat on the log beside me and glanced at Bonnie out the corner of her eye.

"Yes," she said. "It was very...*relaxing*. Those air mattresses are surprisingly comfortable. How about you guys?"

I didn't think it would be proper to mention the suspected 'raccoon' invasion that disrupted the camp last night.

"Slept like a baby," I said.

I glanced at Emma's bare legs in her cargo shorts and noticed a pink glow.

"I think maybe you got a little too much sun yesterday, Emma."

I reached into my fanny pack and pulled out some sunscreen.

"You might want to put a little protection on. Lilly's suggesting we go for another canoe excursion today. You'll be fully exposed out there on the water."

Emma accepted the bottle and began spreading the lotion across the inside and top of her thighs. I tried not to stare, but her skin blushed and blanched as she pressed her fingers into her soft flesh.

"Actually, you might want to wear your cargo pants to cover up,"

Lilly said. "I can tell you from experience how easy it is to get a nasty sunburn spending the whole day out on the water."

Hannah suddenly interrupted us as she traipsed out of the brush.

"That was fun." She held the toilet paper roll up for everybody to see. "Anybody else need to take a go?"

We all shook our heads and Hannah placed the shovel and roll behind the log next to Bonnie as she sat down beside her.

"So what's the plan for today? More sexy stories and skinny dipping? What else can six girls do in the middle of nowhere?"

Emma and Bonnie shifted uncomfortably on their logs, and the group paused for a moment in awkward silence.

"Lilly suggested a little canoe excursion," I said. "We could explore the surrounding countryside a bit more."

Hannah peered around the lake as she listened to the sound of frogs chirping from the lily pond.

"Doesn't look like there's much more to discover out here than pine cones and bullfrogs."

"We can try to track down one of those *bears* if you're looking for a bit more excitement," Lilly said. "Or maybe some rattlesnakes. There's a lot more interesting wildlife out here than you might imagine. Don't be such a party-pooper, Hannah."

"Rattlesnakes?" Emma said, her eyes suddenly widening. "You didn't mention *those* before heading out."

"I didn't want to scare you guys away. I figured that might tip the balance. But don't worry. They'll give you plenty of warning if you get too close. You've got a better chance of getting hit by a car in the city than being bitten by a snake out here."

She reached behind her log and opened a cooler, then held out a couple of eggs and a pack of bacon.

"But first, who's up for a real woodsman's breakfast? Cooked up real authentic-like on the griddle?"

"Hell, yes!" Hannah exclaimed. "I could eat a moose right now."

After a hearty breakfast of scrambled eggs and pan-fried Canadian bacon, we set out in our two canoes to explore the lake. There were lots of bays and gullies in the meandering shoreline, and I marveled at the quiet and serene beauty of the craggy landscape. Some of the girls tried trolling for fish behind our canoes, but no one caught anything and by midday, our stomachs were grumbling again. Lilly suggested we put in on a larger island to forage for firewood since we'd already collected most of the loose driftwood on our own little islet.

We beached our canoes on the new island and decided to pair up to go exploring. The island was quite large with lots of tall pine, spruce, and fir trees providing ample shade from the hot overhead sun. But the trek was slow-going, with many fallen trees and lichen-covered rocks to sidestep. The girls had decided to pair up again based on their previous tent assignments, and I was beginning to despair of ever finding any alone time with Emma.

We spread out in different directions over the large island. After thirty minutes or so of exploring with Hannah, I caught a glimpse of two bodies reflecting in a shaded glade. I stopped and peered in their direction and realized it was Bonnie and Emma. They were topless and making out behind a large tree! Hannah looked back at me wondering what was holding me up, and I told her I had to stop to take care of some business and that I'd catch up with her.

As she moved further ahead, I slowly crept closer to Bonnie and Emma's position. It was hard to stay quiet with all the loose twigs and rocks on the ground, but I managed to get within about thirty feet of them without being detected. When I got close to their alcove, I ducked behind a large stump and saw that Emma had removed all of her clothing and was sitting on a fallen tree with her legs spread apart. Bonnie knelt between her legs bobbing her head up and down.

Fuck! I thought. *She's licking her pussy! Right in the middle of the forest!*

I quickly dropped my pants and began rubbing my cunt furiously. I had to fight hard to control my breathing and movement so as not to be detected as I gritted my teeth trying to contain my pleasure. Emma arched her back and placed her hands beside Bonnie's ears then pulled her head into her snatch. I could hear her grunting and moaning, and it took every ounce of my energy to remain silent.

As I hunched down behind my tree stump trying to keep my head hidden, suddenly a twig broke underfoot and I ducked under the stump to hide from the girls. I could hear them stop for a moment as they looked around to ensure they were alone, then Emma's moaning resumed. When I peered back over the log, my eyes met with Emma's and we froze for a moment realizing we'd seen each other. But she didn't ask Bonnie to stop and instead pulled her head harder into her pussy as she stared at me through glistening eyes. I kept my head down just enough to stay hidden if Bonnie turned around, while I watched Emma get eaten out.

Emma began rocking her hips and as she pulled Bonnie into her, I could tell that she was close. I raised up just enough for Emma to see my face while I squeezed my breast with one hand and jilled myself with the other. Emma must have noticed my movement and known what I was doing, and the sight of seeing each other getting turned on watching the other, ramped up our arousal even more.

Emma stared straight at me as she began panting louder, then she nodded as if signaling that she was ready. That was all I needed and I gushed all over my fallen pants as I watched Emma's head bob and jerk in quiet climax. After a minute or so, Bonnie and Emma began to get dressed and I ducked under my tree stump to collect myself. For now, at least, this private moment of pleasure would remain between Emma and me.

When I caught up with Hannah, she looked at the wet dribbles on the front of my pants and shook her head.

"Girl, you've got to learn how to shit in the woods properly. The trick is to find a rock or tree stump to support yourself. If you're going to squat down, the least you can do is take your pants off first."

"Yeah," I said. "A tree stump sounds like a good idea. Next time."

"I can't take you anywhere, Jade. We're going to have to get you hooked up right soon before you devolve into a blubbering baby."

I just nodded quietly as I followed Hannah along the trail through the forest.

After we collected some firewood, we all reconvened at the beach where we'd set in and built another fire pit. Then we sharpened some sticks and cooked some wieners Lilly had packed in the cooler. Neither Emma nor I talked about what we'd seen, but I noticed her looking in my direction frequently with a knowing smile.

After lunch, we set out again in the canoes and found another tall cliff to jump off, then we cavorted in the water and lay in the sun to dry off. Madison caught a big pike trolling behind her canoe, and when we returned to our little island later in the day, Lilly cooked it up in the skillet and we roasted marshmallows telling more fun stories. I kept glancing at Emma, wondering if we were ever going to have a chance to be alone, but around midnight all of us retired to our regular tents.

After we slipped into our respective sleeping bags, Hannah turned to me and smiled.

"Are you enjoying our camping experience so far?" she asked.

"Yes," I said. "This is nice for a change. It's good to get away. You were right, Han. I really needed this. Thanks for inviting me."

Hannah paused for a long moment.

"Did you have fun on the island today?" she said.

"Um, yes. I enjoyed the hike and the hot dog roast—you know, just communing with the girls..."

"I saw you watching Emma and Bonnie."

"What?" I said, feeling a flush roll over my cheeks. "You mean when I held back to take care of some business?"

"That wasn't the only business I saw you taking care of. It's okay, you know. You don't have to hide it from me. We're supposed to be best friends. If you like girls that way, it doesn't change anything between us."

I hesitated, unsure how best to respond, then exhaled deeply, realizing I didn't need to hide my attraction to women any longer.

"It was just...*hot*, you know? Watching them go at it like wild animals in the wilderness. I couldn't stop looking..."

"I know. Neither could I. You weren't the only one enjoying the show."

I turned my head toward Hannah and looked at her surprised.

"You too? Are you—"

"I still prefer men. But you have to admit, Emma is pretty hot. I've had my eye on her for a while too. I heard you last night listening to them."

I gasped and sat up on top of my sleeping bag.

"You were sure *faking* it pretty well! Pretending to be asleep the whole time."

"How could I? With you moving your hand between your legs so rapidly under the covers and your air mattress squeaking away."

"Why didn't you say something?"

"I didn't want to interrupt your fun. Besides, I was getting just as turned on as you. I rubbed a couple of quiet ones out listening to you and the other girls. Besides, we're friends. I didn't know if you'd wanted to..."

I looked into Hannah's eyes, suddenly realizing how sexy she was. I'd always admired her beauty, but had never thought of it beyond that. But now that I saw her sitting with the soft glow of the moonlight from our open tent window reflecting off her bare breasts, she looked like much more than just a close friend to me.

I leaned over to her side of the tent and kissed her softly on her lips. She shifted her hips closer to mine and we began kissing more passionately, intertwining our tongues in each other's mouths. When she pressed her tits against mine, we both began moaning.

"Damn, girl," she said, pulling away from me for a moment. "Can you believe we've waited all these years to do this?"

Then she crawled out of her sleeping bag and began to unzip the side of my bedroll. She flipped the cover over and straddled my naked body. Then she began kissing my neck and working her way down my body. When she got to my breasts, she sucked on my teats gently, swirling her tongue around my nipples as I held her cheeks gently between my two hands. I tried to pull her up to kiss her again, but she pushed me down on my air mattress and continued nibbling her way toward my pussy. When she got to my belly button she paused, blowing kisses into my little hole, then gently kissed her way to the bony edges of my pelvis.

"For somebody who doesn't like girls," I said, panting in anticipation, "you sure know your way around a female body."

"Who said I didn't like girls?" she said, glancing up at me.

"But you said you prefer—"

"Just shut up, will you?" she said, stretching her hand up to my chin and placing it gently over my mouth. "Lie back and enjoy this. I've been wanting to do this for quite a while."

Hannah extended her tongue and traced a line down the ridge of my hipbone toward my steaming pussy. I lifted my hips, inviting her to go lower, but she paused on top of my mound and rubbed her cheeks softly against my pubis.

"You're so soft," she purred. "Somebody's had some work done recently."

Then she lowered her head between my legs and placed her open mouth directly over my hard clit and began sucking it into her mouth. I moaned and gyrated my hips in pleasure as I ran my fingers through her soft, sun-dried hair.

"Hannah," I moaned. "That feels so good. Don't stop."

"Mmmm," Hannah hummed in assent.

I was enjoying Hannah's attention on my clit and could have come from that alone. But after a few minutes, she started caressing the sides of my labia, then she inserted two fingers inside my sopping hole. I groaned in pleasure, suddenly flashing back to the image of Emma getting eaten out by Bonnie on the log in the forest. I placed my hands beside Hannah's head and pulled her in closer to my throbbing snatch. When she began curling her two fingers against the inside of my pussy on my G-spot, I gasped out loud.

"Yes, Hannah!" I moaned. "Right there. Suck me. I'm going to come all over your pretty face. Make me cum, Han!"

Hannah moaned louder into my pussy and stepped up the pace of her licking and finger movements. I could feel my orgasm welling up inside me and I lifted my hips in preparation for the coming climax. When it poured over me, I couldn't stop screaming out in pleasure.

"Fuck, yes, Hannah! I'm coming, baby! I'm cumming in your sweet mouth. Ohhhh, I'm cumming so hard!"

Hannah held me tightly until I stopped twitching, then she lay back on the foot of my air mattress and scooted her hips up until our pussies were touching.

"Mmmm, Jade," she said. "Your pussy is so warm. I want to fuck you and feel your juices running all over me."

She tried rocking her hips awkwardly against me to create more friction, but I could tell she was getting frustrated trying to generate sustained and steady contact. After a couple of minutes of awkward flailing, I sat up on my air mattress and kneeled over her.

"Let me do this, hun," I said, looking into her eyes.

I placed my right thigh under one side of her hips then lifted my other leg over her stomach until we were in a sideways scissor position with me sitting on top. When I started rocking my hips and grinding our clits together, she gasped.

"*God*, yes! Fuck me, Jade! Fuck my aching pussy. I want to feel you cum all over me again."

"Fuck that," I said. "I want to feel you cum on me. It's your turn to lie back and enjoy my attention. Just focus on the pleasure—"

"Oh, oh, uhnnn!" Hannah panted. "Yes, Jade. That feels so good. Fuck me, honey, with your sweet cunt. Make me cum all over your sweet pussy!"

Hannah began flailing against the side of the tent as she screamed and moaned. I was certain that the whole campsite must have heard what was going on, but neither of us cared. We were so lost in the moment and enjoying our rising pleasure, we would have gladly fucked each other in full view of the other girls right now.

As I listened to Hannah's breathing grow more ragged and her moans increasing in volume, I wondered if Emma was playing with herself like I had yesterday listening to her. Hannah was rocking her hips wildly against me now and tearing at the sides of our tent. I knew she was close and I placed my hands around her hips and dug my nails into the sides of her ass as I pulled her harder against me.

"Now, Han!" I prompted her. "*Come* for me, baby. Let me feel you gush all over my gaping pussy!"

That was apparently all Hannah was waiting for, and she curled her body up toward me and held out her hand. I interlaced my fingers between hers and clasped her hand firmly. I could feel Hannah's grip growing progressively tighter until she finally grunted and exhaled loudly.

"Fuck! I'm *coming*, Jade! I'm cumming all over your sweet cunt. Fuck me, baby!"

I wanted to just focus on Hannah's pleasure and give her a full and proper fucking, but when she spoke those words I couldn't hold back any longer. As I came with her, we both sprayed our juices all over each other's pussies and thighs, screaming and moaning in delight. We shook and spasmed together for almost a full minute as we locked our cunts together in a paroxysm of pleasure.

When we finally collapsed beside each other on my air mattress, we heard the distinctive sound of girls' moaning coming from both of the other tents. We giggled and kissed each other listening to the other girls enjoying each other, then we made love for another hour before falling asleep in each other's arms in my sleeping bag.

4

GROUP FUN

The next morning, we all met around the campfire for hot chocolate. At first, we just made small talk about the scenery and how well everybody was sleeping with all the fresh air. Nobody wanted to broach the subject of what had obviously happened last night in each of our tents. As usual, Hannah was the first to break the awkward silence.

"Well, it's obvious that we were doing a lot more than just *sleeping* last night!"

We all looked at each other sheepishly and smiled.

"I think we should mix it up tonight," she said. "I propose that we change the bunking arrangements. You know, to make it more *interesting*. If we're gonna do this, we should at least *share the spoils*, shouldn't we?"

I glared at Hannah in mock indignation.

"*What?!*" I said. "You've grown *bored* with me already?"

Hannah leaned across our log and planted a big wet kiss on my lips.

"No baby," she said. "I could never grow tired of you. It's just that we only have a few more days out here and we're not going to have too many more chances like this. We can't fit *everybody* in one tent—"

"Hannah has a point," Lilly said, smiling at her partner, Madison. "It's obvious that we were all getting turned on listening to the others having fun. My panties haven't been dry since I heard Emma and Bonnie getting it on two nights ago."

"You *heard* us?!" Emma said. "Why didn't you say something?"

"I didn't want to put you on the spot. I wasn't sure if you guys wanted to share the love. But after last night, I think it's safe to say all bets are off."

We all looked at each other tentatively around the campfire.

"So...who goes with who?" I asked, sensing an argument over who got to sleep with Emma next. "Do we draw lots or something?"

"You make it sound like we're choosing who goes into battle!" Hannah joked. "Besides, we don't just have to stick with *one* partner, do we? We can always move around..."

"You mean play musical tents?" Maddie kidded.

"Something like that," Hannah said.

"I don't think there's any rules for this sort of thing," Lilly interjected. "Let's see how the chips fall. What do you say we work up our appetite a little bit with some more hiking and canoeing? Maybe we can find another waterfall to play in. That should get our juices flowing!"

We all looked at each other excitedly around the fire, contemplating what lay ahead for each of us. When my eyes met Emma's, we lingered a little longer, smiling as we fanned our legs together unconsciously.

"Right, then," Lilly said, reaching into the cooler. "Who's up for some more of that Canadian bacon?"

"I definitely could use a little *meat* right now," Hannah said, winking at me.

We spent the rest of the day swimming, fishing, and canoeing around the lake. When we found another waterfall, we took off our clothes and frolicked and washed ourselves in the warm fountain. We rubbed our naked bodies together playfully under the falling water, but nobody made any moves to go further. It seemed like everybody was saving themselves for the main event later this evening. But the few moments I had touching Emma's naked body were electrifying, and I knew that I wanted her all to myself if I could find a way to swing it.

When we got back to our camp, Lilly cleaned and cooked the fresh catch we'd caught that day, then we roasted some more marshmallows while we waited for the first one to make the initial move. Emma kept glancing in my direction, and after a half hour or so she motioned with her head toward the brush. I understood her meaning immediately and excused myself on the pretense of having to relieve myself.

"I think I hear the call of the wild," I said, picking up a roll of toilet paper and standing up off my log. "You girls don't go anywhere. We've still got the whole night ahead of us."

I headed into the bush to do my business, and a minute later Emma stood up and excused herself too. She headed in a different direction into the bush but quickly backtracked in my direction. We met on the fishing bank near the lily pond and giggled.

"Whew!" Emma said, smiling at me. "*That* was awkward. I thought we'd never find a chance to get away!"

"You've felt the same way?" I said, wondering if she felt as strongly toward me as I did toward her.

"Of course! I've been dying to get into your pants ever since the first day when we rode together in the back seat of the rental—."

I leaned in and kissed Emma hard on her lips. We pressed our bodies together and quickly fumbled to take our clothes off. We side-stepped awkwardly towards a tree and I pressed her against the trunk, then reached down and inserted two fingers into her sopping pussy. It wasn't very romantic, but I wanted to fuck her so bad. I pulled my palm up hard against her mound and began finger-fucking her roughly with my hand while I kissed her passionately.

As Emma panted I could hear the sound of her bare back rubbing against the bark of the tree. After a couple of minutes, she pulled away and looked at me.

"Do you mind if we head back to the camp and go into my tent? It's not very comfortable out here, and I'm getting eaten alive by the mosquitoes. Let's go somewhere cozier where we can take our time and do this right. I want to make love to you slowly and feel every part of you."

I looked into Emma's eyes and smiled. She didn't need to ask me twice. I'd been so wrapped up in my own lust, I hadn't noticed that I'd also been stung three times on my ass. We quickly pulled on our clothes and scampered back to the camp. When we got to the fire pit, all of the girls were gone. We looked around and noticed movement in two of the tents. Emma's was the only one that was still, so we unzipped the front and wiggled inside. We tore off each other's clothes then snuggled together into her sleeping bag to warm up from the evening chill.

At first, we just ran our hands over each other's bodies and held each other close trying to warm up in the soft bedroll, while we giggled like two little girls. But it didn't take long for things to heat up. I kissed Emma on her mouth and pressed my tongue between her lips while I ground my hips against hers. When I slipped my thigh between her legs and pressed my knee against her warm box, Emma moaned softly in my mouth. I was surprised how wet she was already. The inside of her thighs were coated with her slick lubrication all the way down to her knees.

I lifted myself up and looked at Emma's pretty face as she sighed from the feeling of my thigh sliding between her legs, then I lowered my face to her chest. I'd been dying to suck on her little breasts from the moment I saw her, and her nipples puckered inside my mouth as she pushed her body against me. I squeezed her tits with two hands as I moved from one breast to the other, savoring the taste of her sweet, tender nubs.

Emma reached down and cupped my breasts while I sucked on her, pinching and rolling my thick nipples between her fingers. I lifted myself up and rolled my tits across hers, feeling our erect nipples rubbing against one another. I could feel her hips rising and swaying in obvious need of attention, and I moved my head further down.

I nibbled on her soft pubis for a few moments, then I kissed my way across her abdomen onto the side of her ass, biting her playfully on her cheek. She turned her body to give me more access, and I gently flipped her over onto her stomach. I could see her magnificent ass in the moonlight, and I cupped and squeezed her buttock muscles, marveling at how perfectly round and tight they were. Then I spread her cheeks and thrust my mouth inside her crack.

Emma gasped when I found her rosebud and began licking around her opening. I knew she was clean because I'd watched her wash herself in the waterfall and noticed that she hadn't gone into the woods since then. She tilted her ass upward and moaned loudly while I squeezed her ass and licked her anus. Then I spread her legs apart and thrust my hand between her legs.

The soft fabric of the sleeping bag was already soaked through from her wetness, and I easily slid my fingers into her slippery hole. As I flicked my tongue over her tender rosebud, I began to thrust my fingers in and out of her pussy. She grunted with each thrust and began wailing in pleasure as I pounded my hand into her.

"Oh! Oh! Oh! she growled, as her body slid forward and back over the air mattress. "Fuck me, Jade!" she said. "Suck my ass!"

I turned my hand over until my palm was facing down, then I slipped the rest of my fingers into her and began fucking her harder. I could feel Emma's pussy opening up inside and knew that she was close to coming. I curled my fingers and trilled her G-spot.

"Fuck, Jade!' she screamed. "Don't stop! Make me cum! I'm going to cum!"

Emma grunted like a wild animal as she pushed her hips down hard onto my hand and squeezed her thighs and buttocks muscles together, burying my face in her ass. I could feel her pussy and anus spasming in hard contractions as she grunted with each pulse. I held her for a few moments, then gently kissed her cheeks as she flopped down onto the air mattress.

A few minutes later, the zipper on the front of our tent opened and Hannah and Maddie stuck their heads through the flap.

"Do you guys want some company?" she said, smiling like a Cheshire Cat. "It sounds like *somebody's* having all the fun in here."

Emma and I looked at one another and laughed.

"The more the merrier!" I said, motioning for them to come in. The girls scampered into our tent but just as Hannah began closing the zipper, Lilly stuck her head in.

"Feel like two more?" she asked.

We all giggled as everybody piled into our tent, and soon after we formed a giant swirling mass of bodies, sucking, licking, and tribbing each other into the wee hours of the night.

We fell asleep on top of one another around four a.m. It wasn't until almost midday the next morning when we slowly crawled out of the tent. While Lilly prepared brunch, the rest of us went our separate ways into the bush to relieve ourselves. A few minutes later, Hannah called out from the north side of the island. We all rushed to her thinking she'd fallen or hurt herself, then we saw her crouched down, pointing over the lake.

"Look," she said. "Do you see that?"

I squinted into the distance and saw a canoe with two occupants slowly paddling across the lake, on a parallel course with our island.

"I guess we're not the only ones out here, after all," I said, nodding.

"Can you make out who it is?" Bonnie said. "I mean, are they boys or girls—or one of each? Should we invite them over to share brunch?"

We all looked at each other, hesitating. None of us was sure we were ready to share ourselves with anyone else after last night's orgy.

Hannah suddenly looked in my direction.

"Jade," she said. "Did you bring your binoculars from home? Let's see what they look like close-up. If it's a couple, they might just want to be left alone."

I nodded and hurried back to my tent to retrieve my field glasses from my backpack. When I returned to the group, Hannah took the glasses from my hand as we all crouched down on the mossy ground, spying on the interlopers.

Hannah held the glasses up to her eyes and swiveled the focus button on top.

"Holy shit!" she said. "It's two *guys*. Two very *young* guys!"

"*How* young exactly?" Lilly said.

Hannah paused as she steadied the binoculars over her forehead and adjusted the focus.

"Late teens, early twenties at most. And they're cute! Long hair, a little rough around the edges maybe, but buff!"

"I guess we know at least *one* of us is on board with that," I said.

We all peered over at Lilly and she chuckled as she smiled at us slyly.

"Sounds like the kind of guys who would drive a beat-up Pathfinder," she said, remembering the other car in the parking lot of our trailhead.

Hannah turned around and looked at each of us carefully.

"What do you say, girls? Should we invite them over? I mean, I don't want to spoil our fun, but this could mix things up quite nicely. Think of all the *permutations* this could make. I bet those horny teenagers would jump at a chance to join six sexy girls alone on a deserted island."

We all looked at one another for a moment, then we giggled and stood up on the bank of our island.

"Over here!" Hannah yelled, waving her arms over her head trying to get the attention of the two paddlers. "Come to Momma, you sexy little hunks."

We all jumped up and down on the shore screaming and yelling, and the canoeists stopped paddling for a moment, looking in our direction. Then they looked at one another, unsure of our intention.

"Oh, for crying out loud," Hannah said, peeling off her shirt and bra. "I think they need a little more encouragement."

We all peeled off our tops and jumped up and down on the shore-line, our tits bouncing up and down.

"Here we are!" Lilly shouted. "Six sexy, horny girls! Come dip your paddles in some even hotter water!"

The canoeists suddenly began paddling again, and I saw the boat begin to turn in our direction.

Oh boy, I thought. *Now we've really gotten ourselves into a row of trouble...*

VOLUME TWO

SWEDISH SAUNA

1

———

I knew this trip was going to be different as soon as I stepped onto the plane. The flight attendants aboard my SAS flight to Stockholm were drop-dead gorgeous. Not just typical cute-stewardesses pretty, like top supermodel stunning. Every one of them was tall, slim, and *built*. With high cheekbones, full pouty lips, and steel-blue eyes, I felt like was like I was being transported to another *planet*, not another country. One where everybody had natural blonde hair, sexy figures, and movie-star looks.

As I streamed down the aisle with the other passengers, I couldn't stop staring at the crew as they greeted the travelers with perfect smiles and lilting European accents. Instantly smitten, I felt my skin beginning to moisten while I gawked at them like a star-struck colt. When a hunky male attendant in a tight blue uniform offered to help me lift my overstuffed carry-on bag into the overhead storage compartment, I stuttered like an infatuated schoolgirl.

"Can I help you with that madam?" he offered.

"Um, yes," I said, flushing unconsciously. "I guess I overpacked for such a short trip."

As he effortlessly lifted my bag into the bin, I watched his pec muscles bulging under his neatly pressed shirt, with my face mere inches away from his chest.

"How long will you be staying in Sweden?" he asked, flashing me a full set of pearly whites.

With his handsome face and tall muscular build, he looked like a dead-ringer for the Scandinavian actor Alexander Skarsgard.

"Just a couple of weeks," I muttered.

"You can't be too careful at this time of the year," he said. "Wintertime in Sweden can be quite chilly and the nights are very long. It's best to bundle up."

"Thank you," I said, smiling at him warmly.

"Enjoy your stay," he nodded before moving down the aisle to assist another passenger.

When I plopped down into my seat, I suddenly became conscious of how wet my panties had become in the short time I'd been on the plane. A slightly older woman sitting across the aisle from me glanced at the beads of perspiration on my forehead and smiled.

"He had the same effect on me," she grinned. "Do you think *everyone* in Sweden is this beautiful?"

"I don't know," I said, shaking my head. "But if so, this should be one hell of an interesting trip."

I pulled out my phone and pretended to text someone on the screen. I knew it was going to be a long flight overseas, and I didn't want another Chatty-Cathy burning up my ear the entire way. I didn't want to lose another moment soaking up the dazzling flight attendants as they walked up and down the aisle.

When the doors finally closed and the jet began to pull away from the gate, I was happy to have an unobstructed view of the pretty stewardesses from my perch at the back of the forward cabin. As the lead flight attendant provided instructions over the intercom system, her pretty assistant took up position at the front of the aisle and smiled at me. Normally, I ignored these boring safety demonstrations, burying my head in a newspaper or playing games on my phone. But on this flight, virtually every passenger in the first-class compartment sat upright in rapt attention, with all eyes on the model at the front of the room.

While the attendant demonstrated how to properly use the seatbelts and oxygen masks, I squeezed my legs together to quell my throbbing pussy. Beyond her perfect bone structure and pretty updo under her tight bellman's cap, her skin was absolutely flawless. Her creamy alabaster tone radiated a natural blush over her Nordic cheekbones, her ramrod-straight posture reinforcing the impression of watching a model on the catwalk. When she raised her arms to point out the location of the emergency exits, her full breasts pressed against the front of her blouse, showing off her Amazon-perfect physique.

Jesus, I thought, listening to myself audibly panting as I watched her go through the motions. *No wonder men joke about the Swedish Bikini Team as their ultimate fantasy. These people really are as gorgeous as the legend says.*

As I sat in my chair getting more and more turned on watching the sexy flight attendant, I felt like I had a front-row seat at a Paris fashion show. I had the blind fortune of checking out some of the most beautiful people on Earth from in my own personal viewing room. Even my first-class leather chair made it seem like I was sitting in my home studio watching an Ingmar Bergman movie. I was glad the window seat next to me hadn't been filled, as I squirmed between the armrests trying to give my aching clit some much-needed stimulation.

But as I began to fantasize about taking the sexy flight attendant into one of the lavatories for a mile-high fling, the demonstration abruptly ended and she took a seat facing me at the front of the cabin in preparation for takeoff. Soon after, the jets began to roar and I felt the pull of gravity push me back against my seat as the plane lifted off the runway. When the attendant made eye contact with me momentarily, I fantasized that it was *her* pressing against me instead of the pull of the aircraft.

As she politely glanced around the cabin, I couldn't take my eyes off her. Whenever our eyes met, I looked away, embarrassed at my invasion of her personal space. As the heat between my legs began to build and the dampness in my panties spread, I peered up at the seatbelt sign, impatient to go to the restroom to relieve my pent-up tension. Watching this sexy goddess had gotten me thoroughly worked up and I knew it wouldn't take much to get me off. Even though it wouldn't be as glamorous as the usual in-flight fantasy, I'd have my own fun envisioning the two of us intertwined in the close confines of the tight water closet.

But when the bell chimed signaling that we'd reached cruising altitude and could remove our seatbelts, I found myself wanting to stay in my seat when I saw her getting up to begin the meal service. As she moved down the aisle offering a choice of beverages, I leered at her firm ass whenever she leaned over to hand a glass to one of the passengers. I was happy to be seated in the last row of the first-class cabin, with the relative privacy of the partition separating me from the coach compartment.

While I pretended to flip through the inflight magazine resting on my lap, my right hand began to inch between my legs in desperate need of stimulation for the aching nub underneath my jeans. The closer the cute attendant got to my seat, the more excited I got caressing myself under my magazine. By the time she reached my row, my eyes had already glazed over as I needed all my strength to contain the pleasure beginning to consume my body.

"Champagne?" she said, turning to me with a tray filled with tall goblets.

"Um, yes, thank you," I stammered, gripping the sides of my magazine tightly with two hands.

When she leaned over to hand me the glass, I couldn't help staring at her ample breasts spilling out over the top of her tight vest. A silver name tag dangled from her blouse reading Elsa.

"Can I get you anything else?" she said, smiling at me as I blushed shyly.

"What else are you offering?" I asked, my mind racing ahead with fantasies of her jumping into my lap while I ravished her in my quiet little alcove.

"Coffee, tea, juice," she offered. "Or would you prefer another cocktail?"

There was only *one* kind of tail I was thinking about at this particular moment.

"This will be fine for now, thank you Elsa," I said, biting my lip at the temptation to flirt with her further.

"I'll return in a little while with your meal service," she said. "Would you like the salmon or the filet mignon?"

I smiled, happy that I'd chosen to fly first-class for a change. Not only was the food and service a notch above normal, but I had a far better view of the pretty flight attendants in the smaller confines of the forward cabin.

"I'll have the salmon, thank you," I said, fixing my gaze on her brilliant blue eyes.

When she began walking back to the front of the plane, my eyes locked again on her firm ass.

That's not the only thing I'd like to eat right now, I thought, imagining my face buried between her thighs while she sat facing me on the sink in the lavatory.

While I continued undressing her with my eyes, my clit throbbed painfully under my tight jeans. After a few more minutes of anguished frustration, I finally stood up and bee-lined my way to the washroom. When I opened the door next to Elsa working in the galley, she turned around and glanced down at my midsection. I smiled at her, then closed the door and looked at myself in the mirror in shock.

Was she just checking me out? I thought. *What would be the chances of getting her to join me in here? Maybe if I leave the door slightly ajar...*

I shook my head, realizing the absurdity of my fantasy.

These kinds of things only happen in Penthouse Forum letters. There's no way a professional flight attendant would risk this kind of impropriety while on duty.

As I started unzipping my jeans to free my burning jewel, I noticed they were wet in the front. Peering down in the mirror, I saw that a large wet spot had formed in the crotch.

"*Fuck!*" I cursed out loud. "*That's* why she was looking at me that way."

I blushed in embarrassment at being found out, wondering how many other passengers had used this hiding place for release after watching these vixens go about their work. But at this point, the stain on the front of my pants was the last thing I was worried about. Right now, I just needed to get off, and quickly. I pulled off my jeans and underwear and hung them on the back of the door, then placed my right foot on top of the vanity. My slit stretched open as my flaming clit protruded out of its hood.

Gawd how I'd like to grind my pussy against Elsa's face right now, I thought.

I washed my hands under the sink then thrust two fingers deep into my pussy as I began to fuck myself, watching my reflection in the mirror.

If Elsa could only see me now, I dreamed. I had a pretty good figure for a thirty-six-year-old woman, and my looks were nothing to sneeze at either. Would she be able to resist keeping her hands off me, watching me fuck myself like this mere inches away?

As I began to feel the pleasure rising within me, I started to moan, pretending that Elsa was peering back at me in the mirror instead of my own reflection. I was happy for the background drone of the jet engines so that no one could hear me.

"Fuck me, Elsa," I panted. "Rub your beautiful body against me while we grind our pussies together and enjoy our own inflight entertainment."

While I imagined Elsa moaning in my ear and rubbing her tits against mine, my climax suddenly washed over me like a tidal wave as I grunted and spasmed over the sink. With my fingers embedded deeply in my hole, I jerked my hand up firmly against my mound while I gushed all over my palm. I was glad that I'd had the foresight to remove my jeans completely, because by the time I finished cumming, I'd produced quite a puddle on the floor underneath me.

Damn—I needed that, I panted, nodding at my reflection in the mirror.

I grabbed a few towelettes from the dispenser and wiped the floor, then washed my hands thoroughly and put my clothes back on. Realizing that I'd be revealing the stain on the front of my jeans for the entire cabin to see on my return trip to my seat, I loosened my blouse and draped it over the front of my crotch. Thankfully, it hung just low enough to cover the wet spot without looking too conspicuous. Then I brushed my hair and reapplied my lipstick to make myself presentable and opened the door. Elsa was still working in the galley, and she smiled at me as her eyes drifted down my body.

Had my ruffled blouse given away what I was up to in the lavatory? I wondered. *Or had she heard my moans over the noise of the jet engines?* At this point I hardly cared, and I smiled back at her with a flush in my cheeks as I walked back to my seat.

For the next hour or so, the cabin was fairly busy with the movement of the two first-class flight attendants serving and collecting the main meal service. I made small talk with Elsa whenever she passed by my seat, introducing myself and sharing my plans while I stayed in Sweden. When I told her that I intended to get in some snowboarding during my stay, she told me about the best resorts to visit in the northern part of the country. I was tempted to invite her to join me on my excursion, but my shyness got the better of me.

When things settled down after the meal service, she took a seat for a brief rest in one of the jump seats next to the main door. As she opened a magazine, I took the opportunity to study her body from head to toe. Her legs were crossed while she read the magazine, and the swelling of her calf resting on her knee amplified the sexy curviness of her long legs. I could see her dark leggings running up the underside of her skirt and wondered if they were full-height pantyhose or mid-thigh stockings with garters. It didn't take long for me to begin fantasizing once again about fucking her as she sat quietly reading her magazine.

Only this time I wanted freer access to my pussy, where I could feel my slippery slit directly and rub my burning button without any impediments. I reached up and pressed the overhead call button, and Elsa looked up when she heard the chime. She peered down the aisle and noticing the light illuminated next to my console, she put down her magazine and walked toward me.

Damn, I thought to myself as I watched her glide down the aisle. *She even walks like a supermodel.* With her narrow foot placement down the cramped aisle, her hips swayed from side to side as her calves flexed with each step. I felt sorry disturbing her from her well-earned rest, but I needed one more thing from her.

"Yes, Jade," she said when she reached my seat. "What can I get you?"

"I was wondering if you had a blanket I could use to keep warm?" I said, peering up at her innocently. "It's a bit chilly in the cabin and I didn't bring a shawl in my carry-on bag."

"Yes, of course," she said. "I'll be back in a moment."

Elsa strolled back to the front of the cabin and opened a storage locker, pulling out plastic-covered packet. Then she walked back down the aisle and handed me the folded blanket.

"Was there anything else I can get to make your flight more comfortable?"

I paused for a moment raising an eyebrow, then shook my head.

"This should be fine for now," I said with a knowing smile. "I'm sure this will make the rest of my flight much more relaxing."

Little did she know what I *really* needed the blanket for. I just wanted some cover while I touched myself secretly in the privacy of my corner while I watched her from a distance.

"Just give me a ring if you need anything else," she said.

"I will, thank you Elsa."

As she began walking back up the aisle, I glanced at the woman sitting across the aisle from me and noticing that she had nodded off, I pulled my jeans and panties down below my knees. It felt exhilarating to feel the cool gust of the jet breeze rushing up between my bare thighs. When Elsa returned to her seat, I glanced up at her and smiled, then she picked up her magazine and lowered her head.

Perfect, I thought. *You lose yourself in your little distraction while I lose myself in you as I get distracted doing other things.*

I snaked my right hand under the blanket and moistened the tips of my fingers with my slippery juices, then pulled them up and began circling my throbbing gland. Watching Elsa's pretty face while she read her magazine was the perfect aphrodisiac while I enjoyed myself under my blanket. As I rubbed my hard nub, I looked at her lips covered in clear gloss, imagining what it would feel like to have them surrounding my pearl. It didn't take long for me to start squirming in my seat as the pleasurable feelings began spreading throughout my body. Elsa peered up over the top of her magazine, and I looked away in embarrassment realizing she'd caught me staring at her once again. But when I glanced back at her, I noticed that she was still looking in my direction as she darted her eyes between my face and the bump in the blanket between my legs.

Did she sense what I was doing? I wondered. *Had I been too obvious in my amateur subterfuge?*

Either way, there was no way I was going to stop, because I'd gotten far too worked up to abandon my solo entertainment. As I returned her gaze, I slowly resumed rubbing my clit under the covering. At first, I did it in such a way that she'd have a hard time recognizing any suspicious movement. The last thing I needed was to get arrested for lewd or inappropriate behavior. I knew airlines had a low tolerance for disruptive passengers, and I had nightmares of being carted off the airplane in handcuffs in front of my fellow passengers upon landing.

But far from ignoring me or raising the alarm to her colleagues, Elsa seemed just as interested in what I was doing as I was in her. While she shifted her eyes between the magazine and the other passengers to distract attention from her watching me, I became bolder and bolder in my actions. I spread my legs wider apart and began to move my hand more quickly over my mound.

When it became obvious to Elsa what I was doing under my blanket, she lifted her leg and swung her thigh on top of her other knee. This time, I could see the curvature of her exposed thigh as her skirt hiked half way up her leg. While my hand began to move more forcefully under my blanket, I saw the muscles in Elsa's legs flexing rhythmically as she squeezed her legs together on her chair.

Is she stimulating herself while she watches me get off? I wondered.

Her quiet act of self-pleasure ratcheted up the intensity of my feelings even more, as I moved my other hand under the blanket and began to play with my sopping slit while I rubbed my bean with my other hand. Seeing that I was getting more worked up watching her at the front of the cabin seemed to increase Elsa's courage in lockstep, as the flexing action of her legs increased in speed and intensity. Recognizing that she was stimulating herself in full view of the rest of the cabin was an insane turn-on for me, and I thrust my fingers deep into my snatch, pummeling myself as I watched the flush on Elsa's face begin to spread down her neck onto the top of her chest.

I was aching for release, and when I saw her suddenly hunch over and pretend to cough as her body began to spasm, I gushed all over my hand, cumming hard for the second time during the flight. When she sat back up and glanced in my direction, I was still jerking in my seat with my mouth agape. She tried not to stare at me to avoid drawing attention from the other passengers, but she couldn't help flitting her eyes back toward me until I finally collapsed in my seat in delirious exhaustion.

For the rest of the flight, the two of us pretended like nothing had happened, continuing to carry on casual conversation while she attended to the needs of rest of the passengers. When we began to descend into Arlanda airport, I pulled myself together and collected my belongings in preparation for deplaning.

But by now, the stain in the front of my jeans had spread to the size of a grapefruit from the puddle I'd been sitting on, and I waited for the rest of the first-class passengers to disembark before rising from my seat. Holding my purse strategically over the front of my pants to hide the wet spot, I collected my bag from the overhead bin then made my way to the front exit door. Elsa was standing beside the exit wishing everyone well, and I paused for a moment before heading out onto the jetway.

"Thank you for such a memorable flight," I said, taking her hand and clasping it warmly between mine. "That was the most exceptional customer service I've ever experienced."

"The pleasure was all mine," Elsa smiled, placing her other hand over top of mine. "Enjoy your stay in our lovely country. Perhaps I'll see you on the return leg of your journey."

"I'll look forward to that," I said, realizing that I was holding up the rest of the passengers from exiting the plane. "Bye for now."

As our hands began to separate, Elsa pressed her fingers into the palm of my hand and I felt a strip of paper fall into my palm. I looked at her inquisitively, and she simply smiled and nodded. The moment I got through the jet bridge into the relative privacy of the main terminal, I stopped and unfolded the strip of paper she'd handed me.

Hope you enjoyed your inflight experience, the message read. *Drop me a line when you get settled in Stockholm. Perhaps we can enjoy a few more rides together on the slopes of the interior. Elsaflygirl@gmail.com*

I smiled a silly grin as I pulled my carry-on bag toward the exit door.

That wasn't the *only* kind of riding I had in mind for the remainder of my trip.

2

———

After I checked into my hotel room, I started up my laptop and opened a new email message. As my hands hovered over the keyboard, I pondered how best to respond to Elsa's invitation. Had she been thinking the same thing I was when she mentioned taking a few more 'rides' together? Was her choice of the words 'slopes of the interior' code for getting undressed and touching each other's naked bodies? Or was she just referring to snowboarding on the mountains of the north country?

Fuck it, I thought as I began to tap the keys. Either way, I wanted to see more of her—any way I could. We'd already shared an undeniably erotic moment together. There'd be plenty of other opportunities to get to know each other better during a few days of snowboarding together.

Hi Elsa, I typed.

Thank you for your lovely note. It was a pleasure meeting you on my flight to Stockholm, even if it was quicker than I hoped. I'd love to have a chance to get to know you better. Do you have some free time to do some snowboarding before your next flight? I'll be in Sweden for a week and I've got an open itinerary. Let me know if you'd like to get together,

Best wishes,

Jade.

For a few moments, I sat in front of my computer hoping she'd reply right away to my message. But after a few minutes, I realized how foolish it was of me to expect her to pause her normal routine just because we'd shared a passing moment on the transatlantic flight. I wondered how many *other* passengers had been equally obsessed by her and made similar passes. Surely, she'd have her choice of the most successful and prettiest travelers if she really wanted to strike up a more serious relationship.

I slammed my laptop shut and got up to distract myself from my single-minded infatuation. After all, I'd come to Sweden for a lot more reasons than just to meet new people. Between exploring the fjords, seeing the northern lights, and shopping the old city of Stockholm, there was plenty to do during my one-week stay. I'd even thought about staying one night at the famous ice hotel in Jukkasjarvi. But mostly I just wanted to recharge my batteries from my boring life in Chicago. I'd been flitting from one shallow relationship to another and needed a change. I figured the further I got away from home, the easier it would be for me to forget about my troubles. I hadn't planned on being gobsmacked by the most beautiful woman I'd seen in a long time.

After I unpacked my clothes and arranged my toiletries, I couldn't help checking my computer for new messages. To my surprise, I had a letter from Elsa marked only a few minutes after I'd sent my note. As I clicked to open the message, my stomach fluttered in excitement wondering what new adventures awaited me.

Jade, her message began.

How nice to hear from you so soon after our flight. I've been thinking of you too, and was wondering if you'd like to join me and a few friends for a little ski trip. My parents have a cabin near the resort town of Are, and I'm traveling there tomorrow with a couple of girls from the airline for a few days of R&R. The easiest way to get there is by train from the central station in Stockholm. There's a departure around 9 p.m. tonight that will get you in to the village early in the morning. If it's not too quick a turnaround for you, I can pick you up when you arrive and we'll all head out to the hill together. You're welcome to stay with us at my parents' place until you're scheduled to leave.

Looking forward to more adventures together,

Elsa

While I read the message, I could feel my heart beating in my chest as I imagined spending more time with the pretty stewardess. But now I'd have to share her with her friends, and I wondered if that would get in the way of our having some more intimate moments together. But she'd already demonstrated that she was attracted to women, and it didn't take long for me to imagine the bunch of us enjoying some quality après-ski time in the cosy confines of her alpine cabin. Besides, if the *girls* she was referring to were the other attendants on the flight from Chicago, the more the merrier. I'd have my very own fantasy bikini team to play with for a few days.

I quickly accepted her invitation, then packed up my things and checked out of the hotel, grabbing a cab to the downtown train station. I was surprised how packed it was for a Saturday evening, and after purchasing my ticket to Are, it took a while to get my bearings and find my way to the right departure track. When the train pulled up, I was impressed at how sleek and clean it looked. So far, I'd found everything about this country to be beautiful, polished, and efficient. Even my round trip fare for the six-hundred-kilometer trip was thrifty, costing less than a hundred bucks.

When I stepped inside the train, I placed my snowboard gear and travel bag in the overhead rack then settled into a seat next to the window. Everything about the train was first-class, from the spotless upholstery and gleaming handrails to the crystal-clear panoramic windows. Even the *people* on the train looked stylish, dressed in fashionable parkas and fur-lined hats.

When the train began to exit the station, I peered outside the window and watched the passing streetscape flash by. I marveled at the pretty architecture of the multi-colored townhomes and plentiful canals running through the city. Within thirty minutes, the train was hurtling through the snowy forest of the interior, and I soon nodded off with my head resting against the glass.

Three hours later, I woke to the feeling of the chilly window pressing against my head, and I looked outside to see a strange glow moving in the night sky. Realizing this was the fabled northern lights I'd read so much about, I craned my neck to take in the eerie spectacle. The luminous bands swirled and morphed into ever-changing shapes and patterns, like a giant fluorescent ghost dancing in the sky. Now I understood why the indigenous people of the arctic gave such spiritual meaning to this supernatural light show. The swaying bands of color almost looked like a living organism, undulating in perpetual rhythm in the northern atmosphere.

There's another thing I can knock off my bucket list, I thought, staring up at the sky with my eyes agape in wonder.

But as the train continued north, the skies began to fill with clouds, and I checked my watch to see what time it was. The nights were over sixteen hours long at this latitude at this time of year, and I didn't want to arrive at my final destination unprepared. Even though it was approaching 8 a.m., it was still pitch-black outside and the train would be arriving into Are within thirty minutes. I went into the onboard lavatory to check my makeup and have a quick pee, then wrapped a scarf around my neck under my snow jacket, wondering if I'd prepared sufficiently for the cold Nordic weather.

When the train stopped, I gathered up my gear and headed for the station exit. Elsa hadn't been very specific about how we'd find one another at the train station, so when I got outside I stood on top of the steps surveying the parking area. There were a lot of passengers milling about with cars pulling up into the pick-up zone, so I pulled off my woolen cap and began waving in the general area of the logjam.

A few seconds later I heard a car horn beeping and a late-model Volvo SUV pulled up in front of me with the headlights flashing. The passenger window rolled down and a familiar face smiled at me, motioning for me to approach the car. The rear latch swung open and Elsa stepped out of the driver's seat waving back at me. I smiled at her and threw my board over my shoulder as I walked in their direction. When I got to the car, she gave me a big hug and threw my gear in the rear compartment on top of a bunch of other boots and snowboards.

"Did you have any trouble finding your way here?" she asked.

"No," I smiled. "It was pretty uneventful, other than the spectacular pyrotechnics in the evening sky."

"Ah yes," she said. "The aurora borealis. Was that the first time you'd seen the northern lights?"

"Yes—and it was even more beautiful than I imagined."

"We'll have lots more opportunities to view it over the next couple of nights from my cabin."

She opened the rear driver's side door and motioned me inside.

"But first, let's have a bit of fun on the slopes. I think you'll find the *daytime* views can be almost as pretty in this part of the country."

When I stepped inside the vehicle, two familiar-looking blonde girls turned toward me and smiled. I recognized both of them instantly as the other flight attendants on my inbound trip, and dressed in their pastel snowboard outfits they looked even prettier close-up.

"Do you remember Astrid and Inga from the flight?" Elsa said.

"Of course," I said, thinking I'd died and gone to heaven, surrounded by the three gorgeous women. "How could I forget?"

On the way from the station to the ski resort, we made small talk about my plans while in Sweden and what my life was like back in Chicago. The girls said they traveled there frequently, and I immediately returned the invitation, inviting them to stay with me the next time they were in town. But the whole conversation was a blur as I kept flitting my eyes between the three striking Vikings sitting next to me in the car.

When we got to the ski hill, we all carried our gear up to the lodge then went inside for a quick breakfast and coffee. The girls ordered cereal composed of muesli, fermented milk, and strawberries, and I followed along, trying to sample the local cuisine. It wasn't as bad as it sounded, and I soon gobbled down the crunchy yogurt-tasting concoction on my empty stomach. Then we wolfed down some strong coffee and went downstairs to the locker room to change into our snowboard gear. The three girls all seemed quite adapt at getting into their heavy boots, and when they pulled their goggles over their toques in preparation to exit the cabin a couple of minutes ahead of me, I shook my head in wonderment.

"You girls look like you've done this a few times before," I said, gazing up at their pretty two-piece parkas.

Elsa smiled, kneeling down to help me lace up my boots.

"There's not a lot to do during long winters here in the hinterland," she said. "It's pretty much a choice between hockey or snow skiing. And the airline frowns upon our taking part in contact sports. Something about keeping ourselves in top condition for our guests."

"I can see why," I said, peering at the Swedish beauties. "I wouldn't want to mess with perfection either if I had your looks."

"You know," Elsa said, holding a hand out to help me off the bench. "With your fair skin and light hair, you could easily pass for a Swede too. And I think you're selling yourself short. You're just as pretty as any Scandinavian girl. Speaking of, let's get out there while we still have good light. The rides close in a few hours and it looks like we've had some good powder overnight."

When we got outside, the girls snapped on their boards then shuffled their hips forward as they began to glide to the base of the nearest lift. When we neared the front of the line, we positioned ourselves four abreast and sat down on the wide chair as it swung around to pick us up. As it picked up momentum and lifted us off the ground, my pussy pulsed in excitement feeling the hips of the other girls pressing up against my sides.

"So what brings you to Sweden?" Astrid asked, puffing a cloud of condensed air into the chilly breeze as she spoke.

"Besides the beautiful people and the gorgeous scenery?" I said, peering out over the mountainous landscape. "I guess I was just looking for something new. I was getting kind of bored with my usual routine in Chicago. It's been a while since I've been on a trip outside the country."

"Well if you're looking for something different," Inga said, smiling at the other girls. "Stick with us. We'll be happy to introduce you to some of our more interesting Swedish customs. The après-ski scene can be just as much fun as the daytime opportunities."

Elsa noticed my hands gripping the safety bar in front of me tightly as I shivered under my light snowboard ensemble.

"Are you warm enough?" she said, placing her mittens over mine on the bar. "I noticed you weren't wearing as many layers as the rest of us under that thin parka."

"I'm used to dressing for the mild midwestern winters back home. I guess I wasn't quite ready for the temperatures up here."

"You'll warm up once we get out on the slopes," she said. "All you need is a little exercise to get the blood flowing."

She peered forward as our chair neared the top of the mountain.

"What kind of trails do you like to take? How experienced a snowboarder are you?"

"I don't get out as often as I'd like," I said, glancing down the steep slope underneath our lift. "I used to be pretty decent when I was younger, but it's been a couple of years since I've hit the slopes. Maybe something intermediate to start?"

"No problem," Elsa said. "Just head to the left when we get off the lift. We can start out on the blue trail. It's wide and gently sloping, with lots of room for us to carve wide unobstructed turns."

When the chair reached the crest of the hill, we all pushed off while I struggled to stay balanced as it thrust me forward. The other girls seemed far more composed and confident, shifting their weight expertly backwards as they dug their edges into the soft corn while I wobbled unsteadily, trying to keep my board from getting away from me.

"Ready?" Elsa said, flashing me a brilliant smile.

"I think so," I hesitated.

Seconds later, the girls pointed their boards down the hill and began carving up the light powder in tight serpentine patterns, three abreast. I watched them for a few moments, marveling at how effortless they made it seem, but also how pretty their tight asses looked twisting and swaying as they kicked up light sprays of powder, schussing their way down the meandering slope. Not wanting to get left too far behind, I shifted my weight forward and tentatively pointed my board on a diagonal line across the slope.

At first, I was reluctant to commit myself fully into the fall line, but as I began to shift my weight forward and back on my board, I was pleasantly surprised by how easy I could turn in the freshly fallen snow. Before long, I was carving figure eight patterns overtop the trails left by the other girls and smiling with a giant grin as I began to find my groove. About halfway down the hill, I noticed the they'd pulled up on a flat section of the slope and I skidded to a halt a few feet in front of them.

"*Damn*, Jade," Elsa said as I huffed a stream of fog into the cold air, trying to recover my breath. "You know how to *ride*, girl. That's some pretty sweet carving you were doing down the trail. We're going to have to step up our game to keep up with you."

"Hardly," I smiled. "You're the ones making it look easy. I'm already starting to feel the burn in my legs. You might need to give me a couple of days to ease into this, or else I might need a wheelchair to get back onto the plane for the ride back. Something tells me you guys have had a bit more practice at this than me."

"Maybe," Elsa said. "But you sure aren't any slouch. Why don't you go first this time and we'll follow. Show us your best Lindsey Vonn moves."

I thought it ironic that they'd likened me to the pretty American downhill champion who'd recently turned the European circuit on its ear.

"I'm not *that* good," I said. "I'll just be happy if I can make it down the rest of the way without wiping out."

This time I flipped my board forward and headed straight down the fall line, rapidly picking up speed as I arched my body from side to side, reveling in the soft champagne powder of the Swedish resort. When I got to the bottom of the hill and stopped at the base of the lift, the three other girls followed close behind and skidded to a stop beside me.

"It looks like you've found your legs," Elsa said. "You can carve, girl. I was admiring your form all the way down."

"Are you referring to my ski technique or my skimpy little outfit?" I smiled.

"Both. I had a hard time staying on the course with such a pretty distraction in front of me."

"Glad I was able to keep you distracted," I smiled. "I'm hoping there'll be lots of other opportunities to divert your attention over the next couple of days."

The four of us spent the next couple of hours carving the hills, taking increasingly steep and exciting trails before we decided we need a rest. When we stopped near the bottom of one of the trails, Elsa looked over toward me and smiled in a heavy plume of mist.

"Are you ready for some fika?" she said.

Not knowing exactly what that was, but sounding pretty close to fucking, I nodded eagerly, happy to have a different kind of alonetime with the girls.

"Let's head into the lodge," Elsa said. "I don't know about you guys, but I could eat a moose after a hard morning of riding."

"Count me in," Astrid said.

"I could use a warm cup of coffee right about now," Inga nodded.

"Is that what fika is?" I said, pinching my eyebrows in disappointment.

"Yes," Elsa said. "In Sweden, coffeetime is more of a social gathering opportunity than just an excuse to get charged up on caffeine. Let's go inside and rest up for a bit while we get warmed up. We don't want to turn your body into rubber on the first day."

We trudged into the lodge and found an open spot next to a large wood-burning fireplace. As the girls began to take off their heavy parkas and outerwear, I couldn't stop scanning their shapely figures in their tight, form-fitting sweaters. The cute reindeer motifs reminded me of Pippi Longstocking, but their swelling breasts and hourglass figures reminded me more of that other Swedish meme. There was something about the warmth of the roaring fire and the sweat dripping down the back of my neck from the exertion on the slopes that was quickly getting me worked up. As I continued undressing the girls with my eyes, my mind began to wander to the possible après-ski activities that Elsa had mentioned.

"Shall we get a bite to eat?" she said, catching me eyeing up her body.

"Absolutely," I said, trying to quell my churning insides. My stomach wasn't the *only* body part that needed attention right now. I needed a distraction quickly before I peeled off their clothes right then and there and jumped their bodies in my mind's imagination.

As we strolled up to the food line, I once again followed the girls' lead. Everybody was ordering hot pea soup or oven-cooked pancakes with ligonberry jam and maple syrup. But when it came time to order coffee, they all looked at me with a strange expression when I ordered a latte with extra cream and sugar.

"What?" I said, looking at the girls with a puzzled expression. "You guys are looking at me like I just ordered *antifreeze*."

"We don't put all that extra stuff in our coffee in Sweden," Elsa said. "We like to take it straight-up, where we can enjoy its natural goodness."

"Mmm, I get that," I said, glancing at her shapely ass in her tight leggings. "Straight up it is."

When we returned to our table next to the fire, I was surprised how good the pancakes and soup tasted. I was so used to the typical American brunch of bacon and eggs that I'd almost forgotten about the pleasures of a foreign diet. Even the plain coffee tasted unusually good, as I savored the natural flavor of the north African bean.

While we made small talk about our favorite trails at the resort, I couldn't help staring at the girls' shapely figures in their tight sweaters as their chests expanded and contracted while they ate their food. The orange flames from the fireplace cast a warm glow on their faces, accenting their natural beauty. By the time we'd finished our meal, my entire body was burning and flushed in excitement.

"So what do you guys do for fun after playing on the hills all day?" I said, hoping to plant the seeds for some more adventurous après-ski activities.

Elsa looked at her friends for a moment then peered at me with a devilish grin.

"Have you ever participated in a polar bear plunge?" she asked.

"Isn't that where people jump into freezing cold water in the middle of winter?" I said, shaking my head in bewilderment. "Isn't that kind of painful and dangerous?"

"Not the way we do it. We only stay in for a short time then head into the sauna to warm up. It's actually quite refreshing. After a hard day of snowboarding, the cold water actually reduces muscle inflammation and speeds up your recovery time."

"Do you guys wear some kind of special insulation?" I said, not quite buying Elsa's dubious explanation.

"Actually, the best way to do it is in the nude. The less clothing, the better. You don't want any cold clothing clinging to you when you get out of the water. We'll have terrycloth robes ready for you to warm up quickly. But the best part about it is the sauna afterward. Feeling the warm steam all over your newly cleansed skin is absolutely heavenly. It's is a tradition we Swedes have been practicing for centuries."

The idea of seeing the three pretty flight attendants in the buff quickly eliminated my concerns about the discomfort of the procedure. It actually sounded like a lot of fun, and my mind was already racing ahead to all the possibilities once we got in the sauna.

"When in Sweden..." I smiled, cocking my head playfully. "You guys certainly aren't holding back giving me the full immersion experience. I'm eager to learn *all* about your special customs."

"Good," Elsa said, reaching down to lace up her boots. "Let's get back out on the slopes while we've still got some good light. It'll turn dark in a couple of hours and we haven't even tried the most challenging trails."

I smiled nervously, feeling the burn in my thighs when I stood to zip up my jacket.

Hopefully the *rest* of my body will still be able to function by the time these girls are ready to stop torturing me, I thought.

3

By three o'clock, the shadows were beginning to lengthen over the mountain, and the four of us headed back into the lodge to collect our belongings. I was actually looking forward to the dip in the cold water to help relieve my aching muscles. As we drove through the dense forest on the way to Elsa's cabin, I marveled at the natural beauty of the Scandinavian landscape. Heavy pillows of snow hung over the roofs of quaint chalets nestled among the tall evergreen trees, like icing on gingerbread houses. The woods got thicker and thicker, until we emerged onto a clearing with a small wooden cabin at the edge of an ice-covered lake.

"Here we are," Elsa said, pulling her car up next to a broad porch at the front of the structure. The setting reminded me of a prototypical arctic winter scene, like something out of a Christmas fairy tale.

"Let's go inside and get the fireplace going," she said. "You'll need to get warmed up before taking a dip in the lake."

When we stepped through the front door, I was surprised how cold the cabin was as I rubbed my hands over my shoulders trying to increase the circulation.

"Sorry about the chilly temperature," Elsa said. "We normally keep the furnace set just high enough to keep the pipes from freezing." She nodded toward a giant stone fireplace with tall stacks of wood framing the opening. "We prefer to heat our houses the natural way. There's nothing like the sound and smell of freshly cut birch cackling in the open hearth."

She kneeled down in front of the fireplace and rolled some newspaper into little balls then placed some kindling over top of them and struck a match. The material quickly burst into flame, and as she stacked the silver logs over the iron grate, the fire soon began roaring, throwing pretty sparks against the safety screen.

"*That's* what I'm talking about," I said, taking a seat on the mantle next to the fire, rubbing my cold fingers together.

"Can I get you something to drink while you warm up?" Elsa said. "Maybe a hot chocolate or a black coffee?"

"If it's not against the rules trying something a little sweet," I smiled. "A hot chocolate would be lovely."

Elsa disappeared into the kitchen and reemerged a few minutes later with a platter holding four steaming cups. She handed one to each of us, then the girls sat down on heavy armchairs facing me. I could feel my cheeks begin to flush as I gazed at them with the orange glow from the fire dancing over their pretty faces.

"So what do you think of our country so far?" Elsa said.

"It's a little chillier than I imagined," I said, clasping my mug between my palms to warm up my still-tingling hands. "But everything about it certainly is beautiful."

"We'll get you warmed up soon enough," she smiled. "Would you like a little tour of my chalet? We've got the place all to ourselves for the next few days, and you'll need to know where to find the water closet and other amenities. Besides, I need to stoke the coals in the sauna to heat it up in preparation for our polar bear plunge."

"Oh yeah," I said, huddling closer to the fire. "I'd almost forgotten about that."

As I followed Elsa through the different rooms of the cabin, I was struck by how small the place was. With only two bedrooms and one washroom, I wondered how four girls would comfortably share the space for more than a few days. But I hesitated asking about the sleeping arrangements, hoping we'd be able to at least double-up in the small space. I was already beginning to plan how I'd nestle up against Elsa on the pretense of getting warm as a prelude to more intimate exploration.

When we reached the back of the cabin, Elsa opened a heavy door and the smoky scent of fresh cedar filled my nostrils as I peered into a large wood-paneled room. Every surface of the interior was lined in reddish-brown planks of wood, with wraparound wooden benches on two levels surrounding a small metal stove topped with gray rocks.

"Wow," I said, inhaling the smoky scent. "This room is even bigger than the bedrooms. You must spend a lot of time in here."

"Having a daily sauna is like a spiritual experience for us Swedes," Elsa nodded. "It's part of our DNA. There's no better way to relax and wind down after a busy day."

She stepped toward the little stove and placed a large ladle into a wooden bucket of water. As she spilled the liquid gently over the glowing rocks, a hot steam began to fill the room with a pleasant eucalyptus aroma.

"That's an interesting way to warm up a room," I said, my heart racing at the thought of soon lying in the heavenly space next to the three beauties.

"Radiant heat is the cleanest type of heat," Elsa nodded. "Plus, the humidity does wonders for cleaning out your lungs and your pores. You'll feel like a new woman after spending a couple of hours in here."

"I can imagine," I said, beginning to feel my pussy perspire at the thought.

"Are you ready for a bracing swim first?" Elsa said, flashing me a sly grin.

"I guess so," I murmured, preferring to stay in the comfortable and aromatic environment of the steam room.

"Let's get changed out of our outerwear," she said, opening an adjacent closet. "I've got some heavy robes to keep you warm before and after the swim."

We all returned to the living room, where the three girls began to disrobe. I hesitated at first, nervous to reveal my naked body among a group of strangers. But as they peeled off their layers showing more and more skin, I slowly began to undress. Their firm breasts bounced on their chests as they pulled off their undershirts and I couldn't help gasping when they finally removed all their clothes. All three of them had creamy pale skin and Playmate-perfect figures. With nary a hair to be found anywhere on their bodies below their flowing blonde locks, my pussy pulsed in excitement as I stared at them unashamedly.

"Jesus," I said, shaking my head in amazement. "Is *everybody* in Sweden in this good shape? You guys all look like somebody straight out of a beer commercial."

"Yeah—we get that Swedish Bikini Team thing all the time," Elsa said, shaking her head. "I'm not sure Budweiser did us any favors creating that image of Scandinavian girls for North American consumption."

She gave my body a quick going over as I pulled off the last of my underclothes.

"But you're no slouch either, Jade. With your blonde locks and athletic figure, you could pass for a Swedish girl any day."

I stood awkwardly facing the three girls, feeling the heat of the nearby fire burning the back my naked body.

"I'm just happy to be mentioned in the same *sentence* with you guys, let alone be thought of as one of your countrymen," I said, hoping to deflect everyone's attention from my naked figure. "Are we going to do this or what?"

"Of course," Elsa said, handing out terrycloth robes and slippers to each of us. "But be careful as you walk down the path toward the water. There's plenty of ice, and the rocks are quite slippery. You might want to hold my hand as you make your way over the flagstones."

We all put on our gowns, then Elsa opened the front door as I felt a rush of cold air enter the cabin.

"Come on, scaredy-cat," she said, holding out her arm for me. "We don't want to let the cabin get cold again. Let's take a dip before you lose your nerve."

I wrinkled my forehead, then took Elsa's hand as the four of us scampered down the frozen flagstone path to a small dock extending out over the water. When we got to the end of pier, I noticed a ten-foot-diameter hole cut into the ice covering of the pond and I looked at Elsa with an incredulous expression.

"You want me to go in *there*?" I said with my eyes agape.

"Just for a few moments," she said. "I promise you'll enjoy it. There's nothing so invigorating as a brief plunge into freezing-cold water to charge up your adrenaline. Are you ready?"

"I don't know..." I said, pulling back on Elsa's hand.

Suddenly, Astrid and Inga threw off their robes and jumped into the black pool, emerging from the frigid surface hollering in delight.

"Come on in, Jade," Inga said, flinging her wet hair behind her head. "The water's lovely. Come experience the crystal-clear water of our natural habitat."

"Natural habitat?" I scoffed. "Maybe for a *polar bear*."

Elsa turned to face me and squeezed my hand.

"Come on Jade, you're just torturing yourself standing out here in the cold air. We'll jump in together and it'll be over before you know it. Then we can all get nice and cozy in the warm sauna."

There was something about the way she said *nice and cozy* that encouraged me to get this over with.

"Ready?" she said, dropping her robe onto the dock.

I looked at her sexy body shining in the bright moonlight and pulled off my frock.

"One–two–THREE!" she shouted, then she leaped off the dock pulling me into the pitch-black lake.

It took a moment to register the feeling of the cold water surrounding my body as my mind was still in shock at the audacity of what we were doing. But within seconds, I could feel the painful burn of the freezing depths as my teeth began to clatter while I treaded water.

"Isn't it *fabulous*?" Elsa said, smiling at me with a big toothy grin.

"Ye-yes," I stuttered, trying to block out the numb feeling rapidly spreading over my body. "That's one thing you could call it."

"Look, up at the sky," she said, peering upward. "The northern lights are even more beautiful this far away from the city."

"It's stunning," I said, recognizing the swirling green clouds. "But I think I could appreciate it better dressed up in a warm sweater from your front porch with a warm cup of coffee resting on my lap."

"Okay," Elsa nodded. "I think we've exposed you long enough to the natural elements for one night. Let's get out of here and warmed up."

She swam to the front of the dock and climbed up a small wooden ladder then held out her hand to me as she bent down over the edge.

"Give me your hand so you don't slip getting up."

As I kicked my way to the ladder and placed my hands on the rungs, I could feel my muscles shaking as I tried to pull myself up. Elsa grabbed one of my hands and lurched me out of the water, then wrapped one of the robes around my shivering body. As she held me close trying to share her body heat, I watched the other two girls emerge from the pool with beads of water running over their sexy figures. Their areolas contracted with deep goose bumps as their hard nipples extended out from their breasts almost a full inch. For a moment, I forgot that I was standing near-naked in subfreezing temperatures soaking wet while I admired their sexy bodies.

"Come on," Elsa said. "Let's get back into the cabin and warm up in the sauna. I think you're ready for a new kind of Swedish experience."

The four of us scurried up the path, then Elsa opened the front door and we scampered over the hardwood floor into the sauna. While Elsa poured three ladles of water over the steaming coals, the room soon filled with the soothing sensation of the humid heat. I sat down next to the stove, with the other three girls sitting on the two levels directly opposite me.

"There," Elsa purred. "Doesn't that feel a little better?"

"Yes," I said. "But not enough to take off my clothes quite yet. I'm still warming up in this nice cozy robe."

"Feel free to keep it on for a little longer," Elsa said. "But we normally like to take our saunas in the nude. Soon you'll begin to sweat and you'll want to give your pores a chance to open up and let your body cleanse yourself."

As if on cue, Astrid and Inga unfastened their belts and pulled their robes open, revealing their glistening breasts.

"Yes," I panted. "I want to experience *everything* here in Sweden the same way you native girls do."

"You know," Elsa smiled. "I kind of like watching you covered up. It reminds me of our little affair on the plane."

"Oh?" I said. "You remember that still?"

"How could I forget?" Elsa grinned. "That was the most interesting flight I've had in a long time."

"You seemed to be enjoying yourself almost as much as I was."

"I have a little secret to confess," she said. "I had a little help of my own while I watched you."

"Really?" I said, pinching my eyebrows together in confusion. "I saw you flexing your thighs, but–"

"There was a little more than that going on. I had something *inside* while I was rubbing myself."

"Inside?"

"Ben-wa balls. Have you ever tried those before?"

"I've heard of them but never tried it. How do they work?"

"You gently rock your hips or squeeze your legs together, and they roll around inside your pussy providing a very erotic sensation. It's quite an exquisite feeling. I have them inside me right now."

"*You do?*" I said, widening my eyes in surprise. "How do you keep them from falling out?"

"It's not hard to keep them in using your Kegel muscles. In fact, it's considered a good way to exercise those muscles to maintain optimal sexual function."

Elsa paused for a moment, as she began to spread her legs apart.

"Can you do me a favor and play with yourself under your robe while I replay our little erotic encounter on the plane?"

"*Hell* yes," I said, happy to see that Elsa and the other girls were just as interested as I was moving our relationship to the next level of intimacy.

As I slipped my hand under my robe, I felt my still cold and clammy skin over the front of my hairless mound. But as I moved my fingers over my slit, I felt my warm natural juices beginning to lubricate my vulva.

"Mmm," I purred, watching Astrid and Inga spread their legs further apart as they watched me. "I *like* seeing you in your natural habitat."

"Yes," Elsa groaned, rocking her hips gently on the wooden bench. "You're very pretty, Jade. I've been dreaming about watching you up close ever since our flight ended."

"I was so happy when I read your note," I smiled. "I've pleasured myself many times replaying that moment over and over."

"As have I," Elsa said, rubbing her thighs together as she opened her robe wider for me to see her juggling tits. "And I wasn't the *only* one who enjoyed that memory," she said motioning to the other girls sitting on the bench beside her.

Astrid and Inga nodded as they moved their hands between their legs and began to circle their nubs.

"You *told* them?" I said, feigning surprise.

"Of course. We share everything together. You're not the *only* one who likes a little play time between girls every now and then."

I smiled at the revelation that they were all bisexual like me.

"It looks like the only person missing from your troop is the hot flight attendant who reminds me of Tarzan," I said

"You mean *Erik*?" Elsa said. "He's quite a dish to be sure, but I think he prefers to bat for the other team as much as we do."

"You mean he's gay?" I said. "What a shame. I was undressing him on the plane almost as much as I was you girls."

"Not to worry," Elsa smiled. "I'm pretty sure between the three of us that we'll be able to keep you properly entertained during your stay."

"I hope so," I panted, watching Astrid and Inga place their fingers inside their pussies while they jilled themselves watching me play with myself.

"Open your robe now," Elsa ordered. "Let me see exactly what you were doing under that blanket on the plane. I want to watch your pretty body while you pleasure yourself. It's just us girls this time and nobody else is watching."

I didn't need any more encouragement as I began to feel the pleasurable sensations spreading throughout my body. The rising steam from the coal stove had increased the room temperature to well over one hundred degrees and I didn't need any more excuses to fully disrobe. I took my gown off my shoulders and threw it on the bench beside me and spread my legs wide apart to let the girls see my glistening lips.

"Yes," Elsa said. "Show us what you were doing with your fingers under that blanket."

By now, I was burning up inside from the rising passion as I watched the three goddesses touching themselves while they watched me. I plunged my middle two fingers into my snatch and pulled my palm against my throbbing button, stroking myself with increasing intensity as the three women writhed on the wooded benches in front of me. Elsa spread her legs further apart, rocking her hips forward and back while she rubbed her clit in tight little circles.

"Yes, Jade," she purred. "Fuck that sweet pussy with your pretty fingers. I want to watch your body heaving and shaking again when you come."

"Damn, Elsa," I said, feeling the wall of pleasure rapidly building inside my body. "This is a feast for my eyes. I'm going to come soon."

"Yes, my pretty American," she said. "Let us watch you satisfy yourself while we pleasure our bodies. I'm close too."

As I watched the three beauties rocking their bodies on the warm planks, I felt my body fall over the precipice as I clamped down over my fingers, hunching over in a series of rhythmic spasms. With the pressure built up inside my pussy from my fingers damming the flow of my juices, I pulled my fingers out of my hole and began spraying long streams of fluid over the steaming wooden floor. Seeing me squirting my juices while racked in pleasure soon pushed the other girls over the edge, and within seconds all four of us were shaking and groaning in the steamy fog of the sauna.

"Now I see why you were covering yourself up when you left the plane," Elsa sighed when she came down from her climax. "That's one part of the experience I definitely missed. You are one talented and sexy lady, Jade."

"Not nearly as sexy as the three of you," I said, catching my breath. "That was the hottest show I've seen in a long time."

"I have to agree," Elsa smiled, peering at her colleagues. "What do you think girls? Is this the sexiest passenger we've ever had on our transatlantic flight?"

"Definitely," Astrid nodded. "I've seen a lot of fuckable passengers in my day, but nobody I've wanted to get down and dirty with as much as this one."

"And we're just getting started," Elsa grinned. "There's so many other ways we can have fun together now that we're free of all the limitations on the plane. What's your ultimate fantasy, Jade? What would you like to do now that you have the three of us all to yourself?"

"Oh my God," I said, realizing all my dreams were about to come true. "My mind is racing with so many possibilities right now. But honestly, I'd just like to watch you three do your thing together. This is the like the ultimate erotic video, watching three gorgeous girls touching each other. I'll be happy to get in on the action soon enough. For now, let me just soak up your fabulous figures a little longer while I watch you get a little more interactive."

Elsa smiled as she peered over at Astrid and Inga.

"What do you say, girls? Shall we indulge our guest in her little fantasy?"

"I thought she'd never ask," Inga smiled, shifting her body closer to Elsa.

"If you're just going to *watch*," Elsa said, pinching a little string between her legs and pulling two glistening chrome balls out of her slit. "Would you like to try my little toy? I think you might find it makes for a more engaging experience."

"Absolutely," I said, raising my eyebrows as I peered at the intriguing balls.

Elsa stood up and walked across the floor then handed me the slippery orbs. I could smell the musk of her scent on the globes and I looked up at her, grinning a broad smile.

"Just be sure to leave some of the string hanging out your opening," she said. "They can get pretty far up inside you in the heat of the moment and you don't want to lose them up there. Once you place them inside, you'll find plenty of ways to stimulate yourself. Enjoy."

Elsa returned to the other side of the room, sitting on the upper bunk while Astrid stood on the lower bench facing her with her back toward me. As she lowered her face toward Elsa's pussy, Inga sat between her legs and tilted her head up as Astrid planted her mound over her chin. Within seconds, all three girls were rolling their hips in a three-way ménage as they began to grunt and moan in unison.

Watching them pleasuring themselves just a few feet in front of me soon got my juices flowing again as I awkwardly pressed the two chrome balls into my slit. They slipped inside easier than I imagined, but it felt unusual to have such a strangely shaped object inside me other than the usual dildos and vibrators I was accustomed to.

But as I began to rock my hips slowly on the bench, I could feel them sliding forward and back against the walls of my pussy, and I soon began to mew and groan along with the other girls. It didn't take long for me to get comfortable with the pleasurable feeling of the slippery balls stroking the walls of my pussy, and when I placed my fingers against my dripping clit, I felt a jolt of electricity running through me.

This is a little different, I thought. *Why haven't I tried this before?*

Now I understood why Elsa brought them with her wherever she flew. With their unobtrusive form factor and concealed placement, no one would be any the wiser as she went about her duties receiving gentle, sensuous stimulation whenever she moved.

As I watched Elsa spread her legs wide apart and Astrid humping Inga's face while they ate each other out, I began to rock my hips faster and faster watching the girls bucking and moaning in front of me. With Inga's legs splayed far apart as she rubbed her bald pussy with her glistening fingers, and seeing the base of her chin planted firmly against Astrid's mound, watching the three girls fucking themselves in the superheated environment of the aromatic sauna was the most erotic thing I'd seen in a long time.

When Elsa placed her hands beside Astrid's head and pulled her face harder against her pussy as she locked eyes on me, I suddenly felt a surge of pleasure engulfing me. With our mouths yawning wider and wider apart in shared ecstasy, I couldn't hold back any longer.

"Oh *fuckkk*," I groaned in pleasure, my body beginning to shake once again in another intense orgasm. I could feel the Ben-wa balls rolling around inside as my pussy walls contracting rhythmically against them, sending me into new paroxysms of pleasure.

Watching me shaking uncontrollably on the steamy wooden planks seemed to bring Elsa to a new level of pleasure, and soon she also began jerking spasmodically as she held Astrid's face tightly against her pussy. Like a chain reaction, Astrid suddenly became weak at the knees as she slumped forward against Inga's chin with her buttocks shaking like a bowl of water. Feeling Astrid coming all over her face, Inga raised her hips off the bench and began flapping her thighs in and out in mutual ecstasy. Realizing that all three girls were coming together took me to another level, and within seconds I was having my third powerful orgasm of the afternoon.

After we all come down from our climaxes, I suddenly became aware of the ache in my quads from my hard day of snowboarding. I'd been so lost in the moment watching the other girls having fun and

pleasuring myself that I'd forgotten I'd just had the most intense exercise in months.

I'll have to take it easier on the slopes tomorrow, I thought, *if I'm going to keep up with these girls and enjoy some more off-piste action.* The après-ski experience had been even more exciting and adventurous than the vigorous snowboarding exercise. I wanted to save myself for the next step in my Swedish immersion.

4

———

Over the course of the next few days, Elsa, Inga, Astrid and I made love many more times between our snowboarding, polar plunge, and sauna escapades. By the end of the week, I'd experienced every erotic entanglement with the three girls that I'd fantasized about on my initial flight to Sweden. When it finally came time to say our goodbyes, I was sad to leave but thrilled to have had the opportunity to spend so much quality time with the three Scandinavian beauties.

As the four of us drove back to Stockholm in preparation for my return flight to Chicago, we talked about reconnecting stateside, but I never expected to see the girls again. We'd had our moment of glory together, and that was enough for me. I'd cherish the experience forever and carry enough memories to keep me entertained for quite some time into the future.

But I still had one last flight with the girls, and I planned to make the best of it. Elsa and I had talked over the last couple of days about how we might be able to arrange a *real* mile-high liaison, and my body was tingling all over in anticipation of the trip. After I passed through airport security and collected my boarding pass, I smiled at Elsa and Astrid as I boarded the plane and took my seat near the back of the first-class cabin. The same woman I'd met on my inbound flight was sitting across the aisle from me again, and I smiled politely before pretending to check my email messages.

While the rest of the passengers shuffled onto the plane, I tried to keep myself distracted reading a magazine while I squirmed uncomfortably in my seat. Watching Elsa do the safety demonstration drove me crazy knowing she was receiving internal stimulation the whole time from her Ben-wa balls. I cursed myself for not remembering to buy some of my own to keep me entertained during the long flight.

But when the demonstration was over and the girls took their seats in preparation for take-off, Elsa winked at me, giving me a sly smile. Within thirty minutes, we reached cruising altitude and Astrid and Elsa began delivering the meal service. It was difficult restraining myself from interacting with the girls in a more familiar manner, but I continued playing the role of naive first-time traveler to maintain their professional demeanor. Besides, I knew that very soon we'd be able to dispense with the charade and have one last chance at resuming our special relationship.

When the meal service was over, Elsa and Astrid seemed more generous than usual offering the passengers their choice of alcoholic beverage. Before long, most of the early-morning travelers had nodded off in their seats from the combined effects of full stomachs and the alcohol-induced sedative. The girls took their seats at the front of the cabin for a brief rest, and after briefly scanning the attentiveness of the passengers, Elsa nodded toward me and tilted her head in the direction of the forward lavatory.

I carefully glanced around the cabin and when I saw that everybody was either sleeping or absorbed in their reading material, I rose from my seat and slowly made my way up the aisle. As I opened the door to the lavatory, I smiled at the two flight attendants and they winked back at me. When I closed the door behind me, my heart began racing a million miles an hour thinking about what we were about to do. Whether it was from the danger of being exposed or from the excitement of soon reconnecting with my Swedish lovers, I wasn't sure. But either way, my panties were already soaked from the rush.

It seemed to take forever for Elsa to join me in the lavatory, and after a few minutes I began to wonder if some of the passengers had woken up or requested additional aid. Not knowing what to do with myself, I began to disrobe and hung my clothes on the peg over the door. Looking at my fully naked body in the mirror, I began to play with myself imagining her touching me in the private cubicle. Just as I was about to come remembering the sight of the three sexy stewardesses in the sauna, suddenly the door swung open and Elsa stepped inside. She looked at me hunched over the sink with my hands between my legs and smiled as she shut the door quietly behind her.

"It looks like you've gotten started without me," she said. "That's my girl. We won't have too much time to do this while Astrid is keeping watch."

She stepped toward me then reached up to the paper towel dispenser above the sink and laid a protective layer of towels over the vanity.

"Get up on the sink and spread your legs for me," she instructed. "I need to fuck you right now. I've been dreaming about this ever since I saw you."

"That makes *two* of us," I sighed, turning around to face her while I lifted myself up onto the sink, splaying my knees against my naked breasts.

Elsa took one look at my glistening pussy and hiked up her skirt, revealing her bald pussy framed between black garter stockings.

"I *knew* you were naked under there," I smiled, feeling my juices beginning to run over my perineum all the way down to my throbbing rosebud.

"Would I have it any other way?" she said, pressing her mound against mine as she locked lips with me and pressed my back against the cold glass mirror.

"Mmm," I hummed, feeling her wetness touching mine. "Fuck me, Elsa. I've been waiting for this a long time."

Elsa lifted her knee and extended her right leg, placing her foot against the mirror beside me. Her legs were separated like a pair of open scissors, with our pussies grinding together as we moaned in each other's mouths. For a moment, my mind reeled at the audacity of what we were doing, but it didn't take long for me to begin feeling the rising tide of pleasure spreading throughout my body. Elsa had already revealed her incredible flexibility to me in our prior erotic encounters, but this new technique with her fucking me in a perfect split took me to a whole new level of sexual intensity.

"*Oh God,*" I panted as I listened to our wet labia smacking together while we ground our pussies against one another. "Are you still carrying those love balls inside you?"

"You tell *me,*" Elsa grunted as I felt her buttock muscles contract against my sweaty palms.

Suddenly, I felt the slippery balls pass out of her pussy into mine as her pussy began contracting in the initial stages of orgasm.

"Come with me, Jade," she panted. "I want to feel you spray all over me like you did in the sauna."

"*Fuck* yes," I hissed, feeling my climax suddenly overtake me from the feeling of Elsa's balls swirling around inside me. "I'm cumming, Elsa!" I groaned. "I'm cumming so hard!"

As my walls contracted tightly over the steel balls and I began squirting all over Elsa's pussy, the balls suddenly spurt back out as we grunted in unison from the feeling of the slippery orbs rubbing between our slits. We tried to remain as quiet as I could in the narrow confines of the lavatory, but it was difficult to stifle our screams of mutual ecstasy as we ground our hips together on the shaking vanity.

When the two of us came down from our powerful climaxes, I peered down, noticing that I'd soaked Elsa's black stockings with my juices.

"Sorry, sweetie," I said, shaking my head. "But I couldn't help myself. When you passed me the balls, I had the hardest climax I've had in a long time."

"Not to worry, babe," Elsa smiled, reaching into her purse beside the counter. "We flight attendants come prepared for every emergency."

As she began to pull out a new pair of stockings, we heard a tap on the door. Fearing we'd be caught by a passenger wanting to use the lavatory, my heart began thumping wildly as my eyes widened in fright. Elsa held a finger to her lips then tapped back twice on our side of the door, and the person on the other side tapped back quickly three times in succession. She smiled back at me then opened the door as Astrid squeezed in next to us.

"*What the...?*" I said, pinching my eyebrows in surprise. "Who'll be our lookout in case another passenger needs to use the washroom?"

"Everybody's completely passed out and sleeping peacefully," Astrid said. "We've got a few more minutes to have a little fun. I couldn't resist. Listening to you guys has gotten me all worked up."

"We were *that* obvious?" I asked.

"Only if you were standing next to the door. The sound of the jet engines drowned out most of the noise."

"Okay," Elsa said. "But we'll have to act fast. Let's let Jade take the driver's seat this time. I'll listen for any passenger pings next to the door."

Astrid hiked up her skirt and leaned back against the sink, pulling me toward her, rubbing her mound against my slippery pubis.

"Who's wearing the balls *this* time?" she smiled, peering toward Elsa.

Elsa passed Astrid the glistening balls and she slipped them inside her pussy, then she pulled me closer and began kissing me hard on the lips. Although we were standing in an upright missionary position this time, we were able to angle our hips just enough to touch our clits as we ground our pussies together. As I began to feel my pleasure rapidly escalating, thinking our little tryst couldn't possibly get any more erotic, suddenly Elsa stepped behind me and thrust her fingers into my snatch as she began finger-fucking me from behind.

"*Yes, Jade!*" Astrid panted, feeling Elsa rocking our hips together. "I want to feel you cream all over me when you cum. Fuck me with your pretty American pussy."

Feeling Astrid's pussy grinding against mine with Elsa finger-fucking me from behind as she squeezed my tits was a sensory overload. Within seconds, I began climaxing once again as I squirted a stream of powerful jets inside Astrid's hole while we moaned into each other's mouths, gripping each other tightly. Elsa pressed her own mound hard against my quivering buttocks as the three of us groaned in simultaneous ecstasy with the cabin full of passengers just outside the door seeming a million miles away.

When we all recovered from our climaxes and realized what a mess we'd made, the girls quickly changed stockings while I cleaned up the room. When we finally collected ourselves and prepared to leave, Elsa placed her ear to the door and nodded.

"I'll go first to make sure the way is clear," she said. "If everything looks good, I'll tap twice then you can both come out."

Astrid and I nodded, then Elsa opened the door and closed it quickly behind us. Within a few seconds, we heard a soft double-tap and the two of us exited the washroom as I made my way back to my seat past the still-sleeping passengers. But when I got to my chair, I peered over at the woman sitting next to me and she opened one eyelid, smiling at me.

Fuck, I thought. *We've been made.*

But seeing that she wasn't overly perturbed by the incident, I settled back into my seat, feeling the dampness of Astrid's and Elsa's juices clinging to my pussy pressing up against my moist panties. I glanced toward the front of the cabin and saw the girls sitting quietly beside one another in their jump seats with a sexy glow still on their cheeks. I smiled at them and mouthed the words *Thank You*, blowing each of them a kiss.

Seconds later, the woman sitting next to me pressed her call button and when Astrid walked down the aisle to attend to her, she asked for a blanket. When Astrid returned with the cover, the woman placed it over her lap and moments later I noticed her hand slip underneath it as she began to stroke herself between her legs. Sitting in the middle row of seats, she wasn't able to make direct eye contact with Astrid or Elsa, so she turned her head and smiled at me. As I saw her eyes begin to glaze over in self pleasure, I smiled back at her with our shared secret.

It looked like I wasn't going to be the *only* one enjoying a little mile-high thrill on our trip back from Sweden.

VOLUME THREE

THE TOY PARTY

1

"How goes the practice?" I asked my best friend and certified sex therapist, Hannah, over lunch. "Any interesting new cases?"

We were meeting for our weekly catch-up at our favorite restaurant on Chicago's Navy Pier overlooking Lake Michigan. With our busy schedules, it wasn't always easy for us to find time to nurture our longstanding friendship. But I could always count on Hannah to share some juicy tidbits from her private practice during our two-hour break every Wednesday.

"Never a dull moment," she said. "You'd be surprised at the endless variety of dysfunctions people come to me with. Just yesterday, I had a young woman worried about her excessive squirting when she orgasms."

"Is that a problem?" I said. "I mean, isn't that a *good* thing? I squirt sometimes when I come too, but it's usually after a long buildup and during an unusually powerful orgasm. Most of my partners find it to be a huge turn-on."

"That's what I tried to tell her. I explained that it's perfectly natural for many women and that she shouldn't worry about it. She thought she was literally peeing on her partners during sex."

I choked on a salad crouton in mid-swallow and quickly washed it down with a gulp of water.

"Just to be clear, though—it's *not*, right? There's a lot of misconceptions about vaginal squirting. I don't want to feel self-conscious about it—"

"No," Hannah chuckled. "You needn't worry about spraying your lover with an unintended golden shower. Ninety percent of the time, it's just the ejection of your natural lubrication when your vagina contracts during orgasm. As you suggested, whenever it happens it's usually a sign of exceptional internal wetness and/or unusually strong contractions."

"And the other ten percent of the time?"

"Some women expel a secretion from the Skene's glands, located next to the urethra. And yes, in very rare circumstances, one can become temporarily incontinent and expel a small amount of urine. But it's all healthy organic fluid, and in all cases an indicator of a powerful orgasm. Most women should be thrilled to experience that kind of 'dysfunction'. The more common problem is the lack of ability to orgasm at all."

"Really?" I said, watching some dark clouds roll in from the east side of the bay. "I thought that was mostly limited to heterosexual couples where the man doesn't know how to properly stimulate his partner."

"That's common, yes. Most guys can't find a woman's clit with a magnifying glass. But honestly, most of the time it's because the woman has some kind of mental block. Either she grew up learning sex was something to be ashamed of or she had an early traumatic experience. The latest studies show that seventy-five percent of women can't orgasm from intercourse alone and up to fifteen percent can't come at all."

"How do you help them overcome their problem, if you don't mind my little play on words."

"Actually, that boils it down to the core of the problem. They have to learn how to break down the barriers stopping them from achieving climax. First, I teach them that pleasure is a natural part of the sexual experience, designed to encourage procreation. Then I tell them the best way to experience orgasm is to stop trying to orgasm. It's like a guy who can't get it up when the chips are down—they're feeling too much pressure to perform. I encourage them to find a quiet place where they can explore their bodies without any distractions then lose themselves in the journey of discovery without worrying about the destination."

"Alone?"

"At first, yes. There are too many expectations when you bring a partner into the equation. They have to learn how to break down the walls restricting their freedom of expression before they can let others into their intimate space."

I nodded, reflecting back on my own first time experiencing sexual pleasure. It was when I was taking a bath and I discovered how good it felt to let the water from the faucet flow over my pussy. From that day forward, I experimented with endless types of self-stimulation. By the time I had my first fling with a high school boyfriend, all my hang-ups about sex had been thoroughly dispelled.

"What about when they return to their sexual partners? Is there even such a thing as a vaginal orgasm? What happens to the *other* seventy-five percent who can't come with their husbands?"

"That whole vaginal vs. clitoral orgasm concept that Freud first introduced is a total myth," Hannah said. "It wasn't until about twenty years ago that scientists properly mapped the full anatomy of the clitoris. Did you know that over ninety percent of the clitoral structure is actually *inside* the vagina? The tiny glans and shaft on the outside are just the parts that we can see. There's no reason why a woman can't experience a penetrative orgasm if properly aroused and stimulated by a caring partner."

The sun suddenly broke through a hole in the clouds, casting a spotlight over the nearby grounds in Millennium Park. The chrome skin of the famous bean-shaped sculpture glistened in the light, reminding me of my favorite U-shaped vibrator.

"Is that what happens when we stimulate the G-spot?"

"Partly. The G-spot corresponds to the location of the underside of the shaft of the clitoris. It's a bit like the sensitive frenulum on the underside of a man's penis. But the rest of the clitoral structure surrounds much of the vagina, which is why it feels good even when we're having missionary sex. We're all born with the same genital anatomy. It's not until around the third month of prenatal development that the structures deviate into the familiar male and female forms."

My panties began to dampen as I began to think about all the new ways I could explore my pussy with my large collection of vibrating dildos.

"Fascinating," I said, shifting restlessly in my seat. "Do you ever encourage your clients to experiment with *sex toys* to mix things up if they're still having trouble making it work?"

"After a while, yes. But first they have to get in the right frame of mind. It's not an exaggeration to say that the brain is the largest sex organ. A lot of women can actually *think* themselves to orgasm. You've got to be *mentally* aroused before you can achieve physical excitement. I don't want my clients to become too dependent on the artificial stimulation of a sex toy before learning to enjoy sex the natural way. No partner can hope to match the intensely focused stimulation of a sex toy. At its core, sex is designed to be a social activity to ensure procreation."

I slammed my knife and fork on my plate and stared at Hannah in mock indignation.

"Don't tell me you're one of those sexist shrinks who still believes sex is only meant to be enjoyed between a man and a woman under holy matrimony."

"Of course not. We humans have thankfully evolved to the point where we can enjoy sex for its own sake. You know me better than that. I consider myself to be pansexual. I enjoy and encourage all forms of sexual expression. Gay, straight, bi, transgender—whatever turns your crank. Life's too short to be worried about all that hypocrisy about only one proper way to experience sex. So if using toys helps you spice up your sex life and keeps your relationships fresh and exciting, I'm all for it."

"Cheers to that," I said, raising my glass of sangria.

"To *hump day*," Hannah winked, clinking her glass against mine.

"You know, all this discussion has got me thinking. I feel like I've grown so much since my boring marriage ended a few years ago. My sex life is so much more enjoyable now that I'm open to having sex with other women. And my house is a veritable sex toy museum. I've often thought about inviting some of my closest friends over for a toy party. You know—to share the *wealth*, as it were. Would you be willing to give a little talk about some of your insights on sexual health? I'm sure there's a lot of other women who could benefit from your knowledge and experience."

Hannah peered across the table at me with a raised eyebrow.

"Were you intending for this to be a 'hands on' party, or just an educational meeting?"

I paused as a small curl formed at the edge of my lips.

"I was thinking we could start out as an informational forum and see where it goes from there. You could share your knowledge of sexual anatomy and mental health while I demonstrate the latest advances in sex toy development. If some of the ladies want to practice some of their learnings and avail themselves of the available sex aids, I don't see why we should want to stop them. Are you down for that?"

Hannah took another sip of her wine as she peered over the rim of her glass with fluttering eyes.

"Sounds like it could be fun. Knowing you, I have a feeling this little party will soon devolve into a full-blown orgy. But I've never experienced one of those, so count me in."

"Good," I said. "I'll send out the invites later today. Are you available next Saturday?"

Hannah reached into her purse and pulled out her phone. I could tell even before she checked her schedule from the way she was squirming in her chair that she was already committed. She tapped the screen twice then looked up at me and smiled.

"I think I can make that work."

I could barely contain my excitement on the drive home thinking about how I would organize our get-together for maximum enjoyment. Part of me was genuinely looking forward to educating my friends about all the cool sex toys I'd discovered in my journey of sexual exploration since my divorce. But I definitely had another agenda. There were a few girls I'd had my eye on for some time who'd rebuffed my subtle advances. Whether it was because they professed to be 'happily married' or because they just weren't into lesbian sex, I had a feeling this party would tear down whatever remaining walls they might have to expanding their sex lives.

I knew full well that some of the toys I'd be demonstrating would tempt more than one fence-sitter into wanting to try them out right then and there. I just had to create the right atmosphere. By the time I pulled into my driveway, my car seat was soaked in a puddle of wetness under my burning crotch. I raced upstairs and flipped open my laptop, starting a new email message with the subject *Girl's Slumber Party*. With trembling hands, I began composing my message:

Dear friends,

This Saturday, I'll be hosting a most unusual and exciting party. The theme of the gathering is 'sexual health and wellness'. I've invited my good friend and registered sex therapist, Hannah Bristol, to give an informative presentation on the latest developments in the area of women's sexual health.

A big part of this is learning to relax and explore our bodies in a safe and nurturing environment. To this end, I've invited another friend, Cheryl Clifton from the local branch of the Babeland adult emporium chain to demonstrate some of the exciting new sex toys they've recently introduced. You're encouraged to learn, experiment, and dabble to the extent you feel comfortable.

This is a girls-only party. Leave your husbands, boyfriends, and other cockadoodles at home. Dress comfortably—it'll be our own little slumber party. Come one, come all!

RSVP by Friday p.m.

See you all soon,

Jade xo

As I began to fill in the To: field with the email addresses of my friends and associates, I paused after entering the names of the obvious candidates. It went without saying that I would invite the women I'd already shared a private tryst with and those who I knew to be lesbians. But half the fun would be trying to entice my stanch heterosexual friends to drop their britches along with everyone else.

By the time I finished filling in the list of addressees, I'd assembled an eclectic list of twenty friends and acquaintances, all of whom I'd be happy to fuck at the slightest provocation. I paused for only a millisecond before tapping the Send button. Then I tore off my pants and plunged my favorite rabbit vibrator dildo deep into my pussy. As I slid down in my chair spreading my legs wide apart, I closed my eyes imagining what it would be like to watch twenty sexy women pleasuring themselves while the rest of us looked on.

2

———————

By Saturday afternoon, I was already dripping in anticipation of the coming festivities. Almost everyone I'd invited had RSVP'd that they were planning to attend. The only person I still hadn't heard from was the hot housewife who lived on the opposite side of my back yard. I'd caught Alana stealing lingering glances at me from her upper deck whenever I lay around my pool in my bikini. But her needy husband always seemed to be hanging about, and we'd never managed to find any private time together. Tonight, I had a special plan for how I might entice her over to my place.

I'd arranged the guest chairs in a semicircle in the middle of my family room, with two additional chairs in front of the arc, facing the backyard window. One of the chairs would be reserved for the official presenter—first Hannah, then Cheryl. I would sit in the second chair providing color commentary. But most of the 'commentary' I was planning to provide would be more *visual* than verbal. I knew the only way I was likely to get the rest of the women to sample the vibrators would be if I demonstrated how some of them worked myself.

There wouldn't be enough replicas of each vibrator for every participant to try them at the same time, but between the many different types we were planning to show, there'd be more than enough to keep everyone entertained. And unlike most other sex toy shops' policy of offering no returns of purchased products for hygienic reasons, each woman at *our* party would be welcome to share and pass along their toys for the pleasure of the other participants.

Beside each chair, I'd placed a container of alcohol wipes and a fresh towelette so everyone could safely clean each device before reuse. I didn't want anything stopping the ladies from being willing to experiment and enjoying themselves to the fullest. The last thing I did to set the mood was draw the drapes and turn the dimmer switch down. I wanted just enough light to create a playful atmosphere while still providing enough visibility for everyone to watch one another.

In front of my own chair, I left the curtains parted a small crack with a direct line of sight to Alana's balcony. There wouldn't be enough space for someone outside my fenced yard to make out what was going inside with an unaided eye. But using the spyglass I'd often caught Alana using behind her kitchen window, she'd be able to zoom in on the action all she wanted. After dusk, the light from inside my house would create the effect of an illuminated stage in a darkened theater. Everybody else's privacy would be safely protected facing away from the window. But Alana would have a bird's-eye view of me displaying all of my favorite toys.

As my friends began to arrive, we shared some wine and cheese and made small talk about the latest developments in our work and personal lives. Nobody wanted to broach the subject of our planned activities for later in the evening, but by the time the last attendee arrived, everybody was nicely loosened up by the free-flowing alcohol. I invited everyone to take a seat in the semicircle, while Hannah and I took adjacent chairs facing the group. Hannah had brought a small case with her that she placed it on the floor beside her chair.

"Good evening everyone and welcome to our little get-together," I said. "It's great to see all my close friends together once again. We seem to find it more and more difficult these days to make time to commune with our busy schedules. We've got an interesting theme for tonight's gathering, and I've invited two close friends to make a presentation in the context of women's sexual health. I think you'll find the planned festivities will be both mentally and physically stimulating."

As I began to make eye contact with the women around the room, they smiled nervously back at me. I was sure many of them had no idea what they were getting themselves into.

"Some of you already know Hannah, a registered sex therapist who has been counseling women in her private practice for almost ten years. I think you'll find she has some interesting insights and experiences to share with us. I've also invited my good friend Cheryl Clifton, who is the owner of the Chicago Babeland adult store on Michigan Avenue, to show us some of the fascinating new sex toys that have recently come to market."

I glanced toward Cheryl and she raised her arm to acknowledge her presence. Some of the ladies nodded toward her, recognizing her from their previous trips into her store.

"Hannah," I said, who was sitting beside me. "Did you want to start things off with a few opening comments?"

"Thanks, Jade," Hannah smiled. "Jade and I were talking the other day over lunch about some of the concerns many women still have about their sexual health. She thought it might be fun to share some of our mutual experiences and learnings in a safe and learning environment."

She reached down and opened the case beside her and pulled out an unusually shaped stuffed toy.

"I didn't want to get overly formal about what should be a fun subject, so I thought I'd try to lighten the mood using my favorite puppet."

She placed her right hand in the back of the stuffed toy then held it up for the whole room to see. Many of the women giggled when they recognized the familiar shape and features of a woman's vulva.

"Hi, I'm Valerie, the vagina puppet," Hannah squeaked in a playful voice. "While I may not be proportioned to the correct relative scale, I think you might recognize some of the familiar features on my body."

Hannah caressed the velvety sides of the puppet framing the organ like two puffy parentheses.

"These are the labia majora," she said. "Their job is to cover and protect the more sensitive internal parts of the vagina. Though I must say I rather enjoy having this part of me stroked and caressed as a prelude to deeper exploration of my body."

Many of the women around the circle chuckled as they watched Hannah playing with her puppet. But they shifted uncomfortably in their seats as her fingers moved closer toward the inside of the faux vulva.

"These thinner folds are the labia minora. They're even more sensitive to touch than my larger siblings and can get quite wet when properly stimulated. Their purpose is mostly to provide a slippery surface for easy penetration of a man's penis, but I like to insert *other* phallic-shaped devices inside me when the mood strikes. These lips also connect at their top edge to the clitoris and help provide some very pleasant friction during vaginal thrusting."

Hannah placed the fingers of her left hand over a puffy red ball at the apex of the inner folds. Then she flipped up a flap of silk covering the nub and smiled.

"And this is the hood of the clitoris that helps protect this super-sensitive organ when it is not in use."

She pinched the fingers of her left hand together and inserted them into the opening of the vulva, thrusting her hand gently in and out. The silky hood of the clitoris pulled back and forth over the nub as she stroked her pretend pussy.

"Notice how the hood pulls forward and back over the glans as the labia minora are stretched and contracted with each penetration."

Some of the ladies around the arc crossed their legs and squeezed their thighs excitedly together, becoming aroused by the vivid depiction of their private anatomy.

"Many women think they can't come just from penetrative sex," Hannah continued. "But this design is intended to increase the stimulation on our most sensitive organ even from indirect touching. Did you know that the clitoris is the only organ in either a man's or a woman's body with the sole purpose of providing pleasure? And that the head of the clitoris has over *seven thousand* nerve endings—even more than in the glans of a man's penis? So much for penis envy. If guys had any idea how good it feels to stimulate a woman's clit, they'd gladly switch places with us."

Everyone in the group laughed out loud and nodded in agreement, starting to loosen up.

"But here's the really interesting part," Hannah said as she angled her puppet from side to side for all the women to see. Surrounding the vulva behind each of the labia majora were two puffy 'wings' connected to the outside shaft of the clitoris, making it look like an inverted wishbone.

"The clitoris is actually far larger than many of us believe. The little nub and shaft on the outside is just the tip of the iceberg."

She lifted the two wings framing the internal walls of the vagina to reveal a larger pair of puffy tissues.

"These tissues extend inside and around the walls of the vagina and connect directly to the clitoral shaft and glans. The thinner flaps are called the *crura*, and the puffier tissues underneath them are the *bulbs*, corresponding in many ways to the corpora cavernosa in the shaft of a man's penis. They're all part of the greater clitoral structure, extending more than four inches around each side of the vaginal wall at rest."

Many of the ladies leaned in closer as their eyes widened in surprise, realizing for the first time just how large and all-encompassing this sensitive part of their anatomy was.

"The male and female genitalia both develop from the same embryonic structures," Hannah continued. "They don't actually differentiate until fairly late in fetal development. Just like a man's penis, these structures swell and extend fifty to three hundred percent when stimulated. So the next time someone tells you there's no such thing as a vaginal orgasm, don't believe it. A woman should be able to come just as easily from proper internal stimulation as from external manipulation of the outside glans."

Recognizing that some of the women were eager for the next

phase of the demonstration, I signaled to Hannah that it was time for a shift in the discussion.

"Thank you, Hannah, for that entertaining and enlightening explanation of a woman's sexual anatomy. I don't know about you guys, but I'm feeling a lot more empowered about my sexual health knowing that my lady cock is just as big and powerful as any man's."

The women around the circle cheered and clapped their hands excitedly, equally surprised and impressed with Hannah's presentation.

"What do you say we put Valerie away for a little while and focus on learning some the interesting ways we can stimulate our *real* peachkas now that we understand a little better where all the interesting parts are?" I nodded toward Cheryl and she switched places with Hannah, placing a much larger case on the floor in front of her. "Cheryl is now going to demonstrate the almost infinite varieties of toys we can use to stimulate our wonderful flower in the privacy of our own homes."

"Or with a partner," Cheryl suggested. "I think you'll find these sex aids are equally stimulating used either alone or as part of communal play. There's no reason why you shouldn't be able to introduce some of these toys into your partnered sex life to keep it vibrant and interesting."

I smiled at her and winked, happy that she'd planted the seed for broader group exploration.

She reached down and flipped open her case. Inside, was a treasure trove of multicolored and unusually shaped toys. She picked up two phallic-looking objects of different sizes.

"Following on Hannah's illumination of the shape and structure of the clitoris," she said. "Women's sex toys fall into two general categories: internal and external."

She held up the smaller object and turned it around in her hand for everyone to see.

"This little guy may look familiar to many of you as the trusty 'pocket rocket' vibrator. It's only about two inches long and less than an inch in diameter, but it packs quite a wallop for its small size."

Cheryl ran her fingers teasingly over the nubby end of the finger-sized device.

"You can place these ridges overtop of your clit and twist the tube to select one of three different vibration settings."

She twisted the shaft of the pocket rocket and the device began to hum with a soft whine.

"The good news is that you can carry this guy around in your smallest purse and use it fairly discreetly, since it's no bigger than your index finger."

She pulled two more pocket rockets out of her case and handed them to the women at opposite ends of the semicircle.

"Feel free to pass these around and see what they feel like as you experiment with the different settings. This is what I like to call our 'entry-level' vibrator. It's very basic, but it definitely does the job."

I pulled my own pocket rocket out of the pocket of my jeans and placed it playfully between my crotch.

"If any of you want to see what it actually feels like against your clit," I said, "don't be shy about giving it a try. Clothes on or off, this is a judgement-free zone. We're all liberated ladies here and I don't want anybody to feel self-conscious about enjoying each of these toys to their fullest limits. You'll notice that I've placed some alcohol wipes and clean towels beside every chair, so you can safely and comfortably clean each device after each use."

"And that's another point I want to make about sex toys in general," Cheryl chimed in. "Different toys are made out of different materials. But some are more *hygienic* than others. You should always buy toys made out of medical-grade silicone or hard plastic. Avoid any device made out of a soft jelly or rubber. These materials have thousands of microscopic pores that trap bacteria and can spread disease. The other types are easily cleaned with regular soap and water, or alcohol wipes if you want to be really safe. It goes without saying that all of the toys we'll be demonstrating here tonight use the safe, non-porous materials, so feel free to experiment away!"

As the women passed the little vibrators around the circle, some of them held it in their hands experiencing the different vibrations, while others pressed it gently between their legs as their eyes widened in surprise.

"Pretty powerful for such a little device, isn't it?" Cheryl said, nodding toward the more adventurous ladies. "But this is really just the most basic of sex toys. There's been a surge of innovative new designs to hit the market over the last couple of years."

She reached down into her case and picked up a donut-sized device with two pointy ends that looked like rabbit ears.

"This is the *Form 2* clitoral vibrator made by JimmyJane. The lovely thing about this sex toy is that you can place these two little fingers on opposite sides of the shaft of your clit to receive a heavenly stimulation, almost as if someone is stroking you with their hand. It's got a quiet but powerful internal motor that you can quickly recharge using the available charging cable. Unlike the pocket rocket, which uses a regular double-A battery. So you'll need to keep plenty of replacement batteries on hand to be sure you don't run out of power at the worst possible time."

Cheryl handed two models of the Form 2 vibe to me and I passed them to the girls in the middle of the circle.

"This one is best appreciated with a minimum of layers between you and the device," I hinted.

I nonchalantly unzipped my jeans and pulled them down to the floor, then slipped my own Form 2 vibe under my panties. A few of the girls raised an eyebrow at my bold gesture, but it didn't take long for them to refocus their gaze at my midsection as they watched me squirm and grunt from the pleasant sensations emanating between my legs.

Most of the other women were also wearing jeans and were reluctant to drop their leggings as they pressed the vibe gently against the seam of their pants. But a few had come prepared with skirts and summer dresses, and I watched excitedly as they slipped the two-pronged device under their hems and began to moan in pleasure. Unfortunately, nobody seemed quite ready to carry their self-stimulation to the ultimate peak and come in full view of the others as they politely passed the two devices around the circle.

Recognizing their hesitation, Cheryl reached into her toy case and pulled out another vibrator. This one looked like a small egg with two grooves on top and a little O-shaped loop connected to the end. She slipped her index and middle fingers through the loop and cradled the egg in the palm of her hand with her two fingers resting inside the grooves.

"This interesting device is called the *Fin*, manufactured by Dame Products, a female-founded and female-run adult toy company. The nice thing about this vibrator is that you can use it almost like an extension of your own hand. It's great to use in couples play to bring an extra level of stimulation to your partner. It's also equipped with a rechargeable battery and provides a quite satisfying sensation to the outer clitoris and overall vulva area. I happen to have four of these on hand, so I'm going to pass these around for more of you to enjoy."

Cheryl handed another one to me and smiled.

"As usual," she said, "Jade will be demonstrating some of the many ways you can use this for maximum enjoyment."

I placed the Form 2 vibrator over my hand then pressed my fingers under the top lip of my panties. As I felt the buzz spread over the head of my clit, I closed my eyes and spread my legs, sinking down in my chair. As I began to feel the rising tide of pleasure spread over my pelvic region, I opened my eyelids a slit and noticed three other women had unzipped the front of their jeans and had the palm of their hands gently rolling over their vulvas. As the rest of the girls squirmed in their seats looking on, the four of us mewed in obvious delight from the sublime tingling between our legs.

Feeling a bit sorry for the other girls being left out of the fun, I pulled the vibe out of my panties and tapped the button to turn it off.

"I'm saving myself for the *next* one," I winked. "I have a feeling Cheryl is getting ready to pull out the heavy guns."

Cheryl smiled at me as she reached into her case and pulled out a much larger device with a plum-sized ball attached to the end of a long handle.

"Right you are, Jade," she said. "This one has the generic name of magic wand and is made by various manufacturers, but my favorite version is this one with the trade name *Le Wand*. This is a major league vibrator, with a deep, penetrating rumble and twenty different vibration settings. It's not to be taken lightly, as it can set you off in a matter of seconds and can be quite addictive. You might want to be careful about pulling it out when your husband or boyfriend is around, since they might be more than a little threatened by both its size and how powerful it is."

Cheryl clutched the head of the device with her hand and twisted the round ball on the top.

"It's got a flexible neck, which makes it feel a bit more natural and it also comes with a bunch of fun attachments."

She reached into her bag and pulled out a variety of odd-shaped covers, placing each one over the end of the wand.

"This nubbly cover," she said, running her fingers over the spiny surface, "feels a bit like a French tickler when pressed against your vulva.

"Whereas *this* attachment," she said, replacing it with a cap having four large protruding nubs, "is billed as a deep tissue massager. But of course, it has much more interesting *sexual* exploration uses."

Then she reached into her case and pulled out a cone with a large curved finger extension.

"But this is my favorite attachment. It's perfectly shaped to stimulate the G-spot on the inside front surface of your vagina, and it will take you to an entirely different level. I'm going to hold off on passing this attachment around because we're going to have a special demonstration of the internal vibrators soon."

Cheryl turned to me with a devious smile.

"Jade, would you like to have first dibs at demonstrating this little gem?"

She passed me one of the wands and handed two others to the women at the edge of the circle.

"I thought you'd never ask," I said with a wicked grin. "But this time I don't want anything getting between me and my vibrating friend. If you girls don't mind, I'm going to get buck-naked to properly enjoy this thing."

As many of the women around the circle widened their eyes in shock, I pulled my panties all the way down to my ankles. Then I flicked the switch on the side the wand and placed it against the front of my vulva, holding it with two hands.

"Fuck, yes!" I purred as the vibrator began to rumble between my legs.

I noticed it was starting to get dark outside and glanced through the crack in my curtains, recognizing some movement on the balcony across from my back yard. Just as I'd suspected, my neighbor Alana couldn't resist spying on me to get a closer look at what was going on inside. I couldn't tell if she was holding her binoculars, but I spread my legs as wide as I could as I rubbed the bat-shaped vibrator between my legs. If she was watching, I planned to give her a show she'd not soon forget.

Suddenly, I heard some moaning coming from the other ends of the circle and I turned my head to see the other women had thrust their magic wands down under their panties and were gripping the handle tightly as they rolled their hips sensuously in their chairs. I locked eyes on one of the girls, a married friend who'd previously been reluctant to share details about her sex life with her husband. As Heather and I began to feel the swell of pleasure sweeping over our bodies, we grunted and groaned in delirious pleasure.

Most of the other women who were without a vibrator had already shoved their hands down their pants or under their skirts as they watched the three of us tremble in our chairs. When Heather gaped her mouth wide open and began to shake uncontrollably in her chair, I couldn't hold back any longer. My orgasm overtook me and I grunted loudly as I hunched over, convulsing in ecstasy. Suddenly, the room was filled with the soft sighs and moans of twenty oversexed women losing themselves in the pleasure of intense self-stimulation as we watched each other rise to the culmination of pleasure.

3

———

Seconds after I came, the doorbell rang. I was tempted to ignore it, but the interruption provided a welcome distraction from the awkwardness of twenty women peering at one another with their hands still down their pants. I threw on a robe and scampered up to the front door and looked through the peephole. It was my neighbor Alana, fidgeting self-consciously on the doorstep. I smiled for a moment, then swung open the door.

"Sorry I'm late," Alana stammered, staring at my curvy body wrapped up in the robe. "I had to finish making dinner and cleaning up after my husband. Have I missed much?"

I looked down at the wet patch in the crotch of her jeans and knew that she'd been touching herself as she watched me through the drapes.

"Not much," I said. "Come on in. We're just getting started."

I led Alana back to my family room and pulled up an extra chair at the edge of the circle.

"This is my neighbor Alana," I said, not wanting to interrupt our flow with a long introduction. "She was held up with a few unavoidable distractions, but better late than never to our party."

I motioned toward Cheryl, who was cleaning the wand I'd just used with an alcohol swab.

"This is my friend Cheryl from the Babeland store in downtown Chicago. She's been demonstrating some of the latest offerings from her establishment. Make yourself comfortable. We were just starting to get to the interesting items."

I looked at Cheryl and smiled.

"What other exciting toys have you got in that magic box of yours?"

"I'm glad you asked, Jade," Cheryl said. "I was just getting ready to demonstrate our line of *internal* vibrators."

She reached down into her case and lifted up two familiar-looking dildos. One had the traditional shape of a pointy pink cucumber and the other looked like an oversize erect penis.

"Until recently, these were the only kinds of internal vibrators that women had to choose from. One's shaped a bit like a pickle and is made out of hard plastic. The other one looks like a super-veiny cock, and is made out of soft silicone. While both come equipped with a handy internal vibrator, their designs are not very inspiring and, just like a man's cock, have limited functionality."

The lesbians around the circle chuckled, but more than a few of my straight friends also nodded, acknowledging their dissatisfaction with their one-dimensional sex lives. I glanced at Alana and she smiled at me nervously as a light blush spread over her cheeks.

Cheryl placed the vibrators back in her case then lifted up another dildo shaped like a banana with a little bump on the end.

"This is called the *Gigi* vibrator, from Lelo," she said. She turned the device slowly in her hand, stroking the tip teasingly. "It has a gentle curve and a specially shaped tip that makes it perfect for stimulating the G-spot."

Cheryl looked toward Hannah and smiled.

"Hannah, would you like to demonstrate how to properly position this device using your little puppet?"

Hannah lifted her stuffed toy off the floor then slowly inserted the curved vibrator into the puppet's hole with the little bump facing up.

Then she pressed the shaft downward, angling the tip toward the inside front surface of the vagina.

"As you can see," Cheryl said, "this vibrator is much better suited to stimulating the sensitive G-spot than a straight dildo. And the best part is that it's whisper-quiet, so you can use it discreetly in the privacy of your own bedroom without your husbands being any the wiser. Some women find it's easier to insert with a bit of lube, so we've placed a tube of body-safe cream beside everyone's chair if you want to give it a try."

As before, Cheryl passed one of the vibrators to me and three other girls in the circle. The women turned the wand curiously in their hands as they experimented with the different vibration settings, not quite ready to plunge it into their pussy in full view of the other participants.

Recognizing their apprehension, I flipped open my robe and spread my legs apart. I glanced over at Alana and noticed she had her legs crossed as she squeezed her thighs together while staring at me with wide eyes.

"I don't know about the *rest* of you," I grinned. "But I'm still pretty wet from using the last vibrator. Screw the lube—I'm ready to get *fucked*."

I inserted the dildo deep into my pussy and angled it upward, then turned the vibration setting up all the way.

"Holy shit!" I growled. "This feels absolutely heavenly. You girls have *got* to give this a try. Remember, what happens in Jade's house, stays in Jade's house. We're all big girls and this can stay between us. No one else needs to know how much fun we really had at our little sorority party. Feel free to take off your pants and dresses and get your groove on!"

Two of the women holding the Gigi vibrator looked at one another for a moment, then they pulled their jeans down simultaneously, inserting the wand between their lips. They pressed the shaft in about four inches and angled it downwards as their eyes rolled under their lids and they slithered down in their chairs. I looked at the third woman, who'd slipped the vibrator under her dress, concealing it under her panties. But within seconds, all three of them began moaning and panting as they grasped the handle of the wand and thrust it firmly inside their pussies. I glanced at Alana, who had her hand down the front of her pants as the stain on her jeans spread further down her thighs.

The sight of so many women playing with themselves as they watched our glistening dildos plunging in and out of our pussies raised my excitement to an entirely new level, and I moaned loudly as I began to feel my passion rising. Within minutes, the four of us were trembling in our chairs as we watched each other fuck ourselves with this magnificent tool. As I began to feel the familiar tingling feeling spreading throughout my pelvic region, I spread my legs further apart and began to groan uncontrollably.

"Fuck—that feels so good," I said, shifting my gaze between the three women. "I'm going to cum soon. Are you girls getting close?"

They all nodded as their moans began to rise with a heightened urgency and their eyes glazed over. When one of the girls suddenly slumped over in her chair and pulled her legs together, shaking convulsively, I groaned as I felt the contractions inside my pussy clamping against the shaft of the vibrator.

"I'm cumming!" I hissed, pulling the vibrator hard up inside me, pressing it firmly against the front of my cunny.

"Yes—Yes!" one of the other girls panted as she also began to quake in her chair.

But I was most turned on by the sight of the girl in the summer dress shaking in her chair as her mouth silently spread open and a deep rash washed over the top of her chest. By now, Alana was rubbing her clit furiously under the front of her jeans, and it didn't take long for her to slump forward, trying unsuccessfully to conceal the look of ecstasy on her face. Even Cheryl and Hannah were getting in on the action as they plunged their fingers deep inside their pussies.

After we all came down from our highs, Cheryl composed herself and sat back up in her chair.

"I knew you guys would enjoy that one," she said, trying to collect her breath. She panned around the room and made a mental note of who still hadn't had a chance to use one of the sex toys. "I see there's still a few of you who've been left out of the fun. Let's see if this next one might entice you into the fold, in a manner of speaking."

She reached down into her bag and lifted up another large penis-shaped dildo. But this time, two projections looking like little fingers protruded from the device about halfway up the shaft.

"Some of you ladies might recognize this little baby made famous by Samantha on Sex in the City. It's called the *Rabbit* because of these cute little ears that stick out from the side of the vibrator. But this device can stimulate you in so many other ways."

She flipped on the switch at the base of the unit and little chrome-colored beads began circulating around the middle of the translucent shaft. "These rotating balls provide quite a lovely sensation when you have it inserted inside you." She flicked another switch and the tip of the vibrator began rolling like a bobble head. "This vibrator might not be curved like the *Gigi*, but if you angle it properly inside your vagina, the twisting head does almost as good a job stimulating your G-spot."

Many of the women around the circle nodded, having had first-hand experience with the toy.

"But the best thing about this vibrator are these little rabbit ears," Cheryl said, flicking the two flexible flaps on the side of the device. "If you place them directly over your nub, you can get a full-body orgasm from the simultaneous stimulation of your inner and external clitoris. There's a reason why this is a staple in just about every woman's bedroom—it's the definitive multipurpose dildo for today's liberated woman. I've got two more of these to share with the girls who haven't yet had a turn, and I know Jade also keeps one of her own in her private collection."

I smiled at Cheryl as I pulled my brightly colored rabbit vibrator out of my bag resting on the floor.

"Damn straight, girl," I said. "This is my number one vibrator whenever I go on vacation, and I also keep it handy in the night table right beside my bed. This little guy has given me many an intense orgasm over the years. It's quite a special little toy. Although in this case—" I smirked, stroking the shaft, "it's not so *little*."

The girls laughed as I switched on my Rabbit and it began to whirl and roll like some kind of possessed robot-cock. Cheryl handed the other two vibrators to the women near the middle of the group, and I was disappointed not to see one of them passed to Alana. But I knew we still had a couple more toys to show, and I was confident that by the end of the evening she'd be fully participating like the rest of the girls. I was glad to see another one of my straight girlfriends holding one of the rabbit vibrators in her hand, and she looked at me devilishly as she smiled with a wide grin.

"You might want to use a bit of lube with this one," I said, looking at my gyrating vibrator in mock trepidation. "It's considerably bigger and girthier than the others, and you might find it slides in a little easier with a bit of help."

I picked up my tube of lube on the floor and squirted a healthy dollop up and down the shaft of the device, placing a few extra drops on the wide head. Then I placed the dildo between my legs and ran it up and down the inside of my labia to entice the other women to take off their clothes. Within seconds, the other two women had taken off their jeans and panties and were mimicking the movement of the dildo between their legs. As I watched their chests beginning to rise and fall in pleasure, I inserted my Rabbit into my hole and slowly pressed it further inside until the rabbit ears rested against my clit. When I felt the fingers trilling against my button, I sloped down in my chair, grasping the end of the dildo with two hands.

"This is one hell of a magic cock, don't you think ladies?" I grinned. "Who needs a man when you've got one of these to play with."

By now the other two women had inserted their Rabbits deep into their pussies and were nodding vigorously in agreement. The sight of two big vibrating dildos planted deep inside their snatches was an incredible turn-on, and by now almost all the other women had removed their clothing and were jilling themselves unabashedly as they watched the three of us fucking ourselves with our big vibrating cocks. I glanced over at Alana and saw that her jeans were now resting around the base of her ankles with her fingers rotating under the front of her panties. I smiled at her and nodded, moaning approvingly at her loosening inhibitions.

I was still buzzing from my last orgasm, and it didn't take long for the feeling of impending climax to spread over my body as I watched the rest of the girls grunting in their chairs. But this time I didn't want to come so fast that I couldn't enjoy everybody else's experience to the fullest. I bit my lip and pulled the vibrator slightly away from my clit, concentrating on the feeling of the rotating beads and gyrating head moving inside me.

I wasn't sure if the other two girls had used a Rabbit before, but from the expression on their faces, they looked like they were having a transcendental experience. As their passion began to rise, I watched their bodies progressively tense up as they gripped the shaft of their big dildos with two hands and pulled it harder against their vulvas. I could see the rabbit ears flapping against their clits as they thrust the vibrating cock harder and harder inside their pussies until they both began to whine at the onset of a powerful orgasm.

"That's right," I encouraged, "let it go, girls. Let me watch you cum all over your big dildos. I'm going to cum with you."

Suddenly, the three of us wailed out loud as a powerful orgasm washed over us while we held the big dildos tightly against our vulvas, our legs stretched out in front of us, convulsing in a long simultaneous orgasm. I heard a squeal coming from the other end of the circle and I turned my head just in time to see Alana thrusting her fingers deep inside her cunny as she mimicked our action, lost in her own powerful orgasm. I smiled at her as we both shook deliriously in our chairs.

4

———————

It was hard to imagine getting any higher than this from any other of Cheryl's toys, but she smiled at me with a devious grin as she pulled her dripping fingers out of her panties. I was a little disappointed that she hadn't yet removed all of her clothes like most of the other ladies, but I guessed she wanted to maintain some degree of modesty while she continued her demonstration. After pausing a while for everyone to recover from their last episode, she reached down into her case and lifted up a U-shaped device with two flattened ends.

"I know you're all probably thinking it can't possibly get any more intense than that," she said. "But I've been saving the best for last. This interesting little device was developed by a woman who wanted to feel something different from the typical vibrator. It's called the *Osé*, by Lora DiCarlo. Unlike just about every other sex toy, this one doesn't have a conventional vibrating motor. Instead, it *undulates*, mimicking the feeling of a human touch on your vulva."

She turned on the device and it began to writhe in her hand like an animated snake.

"This end of the device flexes in a *come-hither* motion as if your partner is drawing his or her fingers gently against the inside of your G-spot.

Every woman, including myself, leaned in and squinted their eyes, mesmerized by the unusual movement of the toy.

"At the same time," Cheryl continued, "this end of the device slithers with a *pulsing* motion that mimics the feeling of a tongue licking the glans and shaft of your outer clit."

"Holy shit!" I said, shocked at the innovative design of the toy.

Cheryl turned her head toward me and nodded.

"Even *Jade* hasn't tried this one yet. It's just literally come onto the market and we're one of the few stores to be given exclusive distribution rights. Since none of you have tried it yet, I'm going to take the liberty of showing you how it works *myself* before I hand out a few extra models."

Cheryl lifted her hips off her chair and slipped her panties down to the floor, then raised her feet to shed the lower half of her clothes.

"As you can see," she said, holding the device directly in front of her separated legs. "This toy is shaped in the form of a 'U' and can be used hands-free once properly inserted. The fatter end goes inside and the thinner part rests on top of your outer clit."

She angled the device so the bottom of the U was facing the circle of women, then she inserted one end into her hole. As she gently pressed it upward, the thinner end slid up her vulva until it rested firmly over her clitoral shaft.

"There are two buttons on the bottom edge of the Osé that you can use to easily adjust the pace of the undulations."

She placed two fingers on the bottom of the U and tapped each one in turn.

"The button with the *Plus* symbol on the right-hand side increases the speed and the button with the *Minus* symbol beside it lowers the speed. But you won't notice a buzzing or throbbing sensation like the other vibrators. The buttons simply change the pace and rhythm of the undulations, much like your partner does when he or she adjusts the way they're licking and stroking you."

I could hear a gentle hum emanating from between Cheryl's legs as she spread her thighs apart and closed her eyes, concentrating on the feelings inside her.

"Before I get too lost in the pleasure provided by this incredible toy," she said, briefly opening her eyes, "I'm going to pass out three more models to the group. Please hand them along to those who haven't yet had a chance to test one of our vibrators. If I'm doing my math right, this last toy should cover the remaining girls who haven't yet had a try. But don't worry, ladies—you'll be glad you saved yourself until the end. This is one amazing sex toy that you won't soon forget."

Cheryl handed me three Osé toys, and I passed one to Alana and one to my straight friend Barb, keeping the last one for myself.

"You know what might be kind of fun this time," I smiled, noticing a few of the girls still partially covered up. "Is if we remove *all* of our clothing so we can watch and enjoy each other fully unencumbered with any camouflage. I don't know about the rest of you guys, but I get just as turned on *watching* your bodies as I do by touching myself. If you're all feeling comfortable enough, let's shed the rest of our trappings and revel in the beauty of our feminine bodies!"

It didn't take long for every single woman around the room to take off the last vestiges of their clothing. Even Alana had dispensed with the last of her inhibitions as she pulled off her blouse and unclasped her bra behind her back. I panned around the semicircle, admiring the different shapes and sizes of all the sexy women.

"Let's get started then, shall we?" I said, winking at my friends.

Some of the girls still had a few of the earlier models of the sex toys resting beside their chairs and they picked them up as the three of us began to insert the curved Osé into our pussies. Those who didn't have access to a toy spread their legs wide apart and began to massage their clits with their fingers.

It felt strange slipping the unusual-shaped device inside my pussy, but as I pressed it further and further inside me, I hummed in satisfaction at the way it gripped my crotch. I almost felt like someone was cupping their hand over my vulva with their fingers touching my G-spot on the inside and their thumb resting over my clit on the outside. But when I tapped the On button at the base of the device, my eyes flew open in surprise.

Just as Cheryl had suggested, the sensation was unlike any other vibrator I'd previously used. Instead of a concentrated vibration sensation, the two ends of the device rolled and undulated against my tissues in a most natural way. On the inside, the long end curved and stroked me in a come-hither motion. On the outside, the other end undulated over my bulb, teasing and caressing my clit with its animated tongue-like action. I looked at the other two girls who had the Osé embedded in their pussies, and they had an equally incredulous expression on their faces.

I smiled at Alana, and she responded by spreading her legs further apart. I noticed the juices coating the inside of her thighs as she rolled her hips sensuously on her chair and locked eyes with me. The otherworldly feeling of someone touching me in my most sensitive areas was driving me insane, and for a brief moment, I fantasized about our two bodies pressed together so we could enjoy the feeling in unison. I knew this was likely the first time she'd had sex openly in the presence of other women, and it didn't take long for her to begin thrashing and moaning as she watched me and the other girls enjoying themselves. After only a few minutes of stimulation from her new sex toy, she suddenly threw her head back and screamed as her thighs began flapping together from the intense contractions washing over her. Not long after, Barb groaned equally loud as she shook violently in her chair from the orgasm taking control of her.

Within seconds, virtually everyone around the room including Cheryl and Hannah were squealing and shaking from the most erotic show any of us had ever witnessed. I was the last one to shoot off, and as I grabbed each of my tits in my hands, I gushed all the juices that I'd been building up inside my pussy out the two sides of my ring all over Cheryl and Barb, sitting directly in front of me. I sat convulsing in my chair for almost a full sixty seconds as the rest of the women watched in amazement. When I finally slumped forward in my chair, completely spent and exhausted, everyone stood up and clapped with a standing ovation.

5

After the three of us who'd used the Osé vibrator had come down from our highs, everybody looked at one another wondering what to do next. We were all dripping wet and buck naked, and nobody was in a hurry to end the party. But Cheryl had shared with me how she planned to step up each activity, and I knew she had one last trick up her sleeve that would bring everyone together in the end.

"That was fun, wasn't it?" she said, breaking the awkward silence. "It looked like some of you shared a pretty intense connection during that last demonstration. With that idea in mind, I had a few more toys to show you that were specially designed for multiple partner enjoyment."

She suddenly stood up and walked behind the sofa positioned against the far wall. She lifted an ottoman-sized object draped in a bedsheet off the floor and placed it in the center of the arc between the main group and our two chairs. Then she pulled off the cover with a flourish and threw it behind her. The device looked like a squat pommel horse, but in place of a saddle in the middle of the curved midsection were two diamond-shaped dildos pointing up about one foot apart.

"This strange contraption," Cheryl said, "is the *Sybian Sex Machine*, and it delivers quite a ride. It can be used by one or two people at a time, but as you can see from the double dildos positioned on top, it's best enjoyed as a partnered activity. Each person can face one another and caress the other as they receive powerful internal stimulation from the uniquely shaped dildos. The secure base of the unit allows both participants to ride the machine cow-girl style."

I panned around the circle and noticed the women looking at the device slack-jawed with wide eyes. It was obvious that few of them had seen or tried anything like it, but their erect nipples and swiveling hips suggested they were eager to give it a try.

"Those of you who like to have sex with a man once in a while," Cheryl smiled, "know that the girl-on-top position during intercourse allows for better control and provides a nice firm surface to rub your clits on. You'll notice this device comes with a vibrating pad under each dildo that delivers full-body stimulation to your entire vulva region. You really have to try it to appreciate it. Who'd like to volunteer to be our first test subjects?"

A few girls raised their arms and Cheryl pointed toward two women she recognized from their earlier trips into her store with their husbands. I was unsure if she purposely chose two straight girls to help break down their inhibitions about trying same-sex lovemaking, but I was nevertheless thrilled to see Dawn and Julie approach the device. They both had tight, athletic figures and I'd long fantasized about fucking one or both of them whenever we'd been out on group playdates together. I crossed my arms over my chest and pinched my nipples as I rubbed my legs together in anticipation of watching the two girls try the sexy machine.

"All you have to do is straddle the device," Cheryl instructed, leaning back in her chair holding a control box wired to the base of the unit. "Then sit down gently as you ease the dildos inside of you, facing one another. You might want to place a little lube on them first to make it go in a little easier."

She handed each woman a tube of lube and they generously lathered the dildos underneath them before sitting down over the plugs. The sight of the glistening phalluses disappearing into their neatly shaved snatches made the hairs on the side of my arms stand up on end. Suddenly I became aware of how wet my chair cushion had become as I watched the two women.

"How does that feel?" Cheryl said to the women.

They both made a soft mewing sound as they peered silently at Cheryl, afraid to look at one another and acknowledge that their naked bodies were mere inches apart.

"Can you feel the bulge in the middle of the plugs?" she asked. "They're designed to provide better stimulation of your G-spot once the action gets going."

"Um-hmm," Dawn nodded.

"Yup," Julie replied curtly.

"Let's see if we can make it a little more interesting," Cheryl said as she began to twist one of the dials on the control box.

A soft hum began to emanate from inside the machine, and the two women's eyes widened as they began to roll their hips unconsciously over the seat.

"Better?" Cheryl asked.

"Yes," Dawn panted, closing her eyes to concentrate on the buzzing feeling inside her.

"We've only *begun* to experience what this device can do," Cheryl winked.

She turned another knob on the control box, and the pads under the base of the dildos began to flap against the girls' clits. Julie gasped as she placed her hands behind her on the bench, unsure where to put her arms. Dawn crossed her arms nervously over her chest as she grunted and flitted her eyelids in pleasure.

"Feel free to touch one another," Cheryl said, trying to get the girls to loosen up and become more engaged with one another. "The whole point of this device is to revel in each other's pleasure and make it an interactive experience."

Dawn reached out tentatively and cupped each of Julie's trembling tits in her palms. Julie leaned forward and placed her arms around Dawn's back then the two women pressed their bodies together.

"There we go," Cheryl nodded. "Feel the pleasure coursing through each other's bodies as you caress one another. Lose yourself in the experience as you become one. We're going to begin ramping up the intensity level now."

She twisted both knobs further to the right then flicked a switch on the side. Each of the dildos suddenly began gyrating inside the women's pussies, pressing more firmly against the front of their tunnels. Both women groaned and locked lips, probing their tongues inside each other's mouths. As they began to mash their breasts together and moan in unison from the incredible sensation enveloping their pussies, I glanced around the room.

All the other women were playing with themselves in one form or another as they watched the sexy show in front of them. For my part, the sight of two straight girls rubbing their bodies together as they were being remotely stimulated by an innocent bystander was too much to resist. I picked up my rabbit vibrator off the floor and flicked the speed to max as I jammed it inside my pussy, pulling it hard against my tingling button.

"That's what I'm talking about," Cheryl purred, watching the two women beginning to lose themselves in each other's passion. "Are you ready to take it to the penultimate level?"

"Mmm-hmm," the two women nodded as they ran their hands over each other's bodies while they continued to kiss passionately.

Cheryl twisted the two dials to their maximum setting, and the hum inside the machine deepened as the flaps under their pussies began to flap wildly. Dawn and Julie pressed their hips forward, gyrating their hips together as they got closer and closer toward climax. Within seconds, they began wailing in tandem as their bodies shook violently with their arms clasped tightly around each other. Seeing the two women coming together soon put me over the edge also as my pussy clamped tightly over the vibrating shaft of my

Rabbit toy. I glanced over at Alana and noticed that she was holding a Form 2 vibrator over her clit while she quaked in her chair watching the other women in the room jilling themselves as they took in the action.

6

————————

After everyone had finished coming once again, Cheryl looked at the two girls still sitting on the now-silent Sybian machine.

"What do you think, ladies?" she said. "Does that feel anything like riding your husbands on top?"

"Fuck no!" Dawn said. "This is way better!"

Julie nodded enthusiastically in agreement, and everybody around the room laughed out loud.

"Well at least now you know how much fun it can be to play with some of your own kind," Cheryl said. "And while we're on that subject, I'd like to demonstrate a couple of toys that will allow you to be even *more* actively engaged with your same-sex partners." She peered at Dawn and Julie and smiled. "You guys are welcome to stay there if you wish or return to your seats for this next demonstration."

The two women kissed each other one last time then eased themselves off the bench, revealing two glistening, pearly-white dildos. When they returned to their seats, I noticed they were holding hands beside one another. I smiled at their new special friendship and nodded at them approvingly.

Cheryl moved the Sybian machine off to the side of the circle then reached back down into her display case. When she sat up, she revealed a giant flexible dildo with a raised ring running around the middle of the shaft.

"This is a two-sided or double dildo," she said, running her fingers over the two ends of the object shaped in the form of the head of a man's penis. "As you can see, it's a little longer than a regular man's cock and it has two heads for double the pleasure. Perhaps *most* interesting though, is this raised band in the middle."

She squeezed the shaft near the center and the band began flapping like the pads on the Sybian machine.

"When two women press this dildo inside them from opposite ends, the vibrating ring in the middle provides some very pleasant supplemental stimulation as they grind their pussies together. Unlike the Sybian machine, which you experience in more of a passive role, with this device you can actively fuck each other in a multitude of positions."

Cheryl looked around the room and smiled mischievously.

"Who'd like to give this one a try?"

Two of my lesbian friends raised their hands but I quickly preempted them. Watching Cheryl demonstrate her toys all this time had gotten me seriously worked up and I jumped at this opportunity to have some fun with her.

"I notice that *you* haven't yet had a chance to use any of your toys today, Cheryl," I said. "If you're game, I'd be happy to demonstrate this one for the rest of the group with your participation."

"I thought you'd never ask," Cheryl said, winking at me. "Let's get down on the floor and show these ladies how two lesbian women can get it on."

I lay down on the carpet in front of the chairs with my hips facing up and spread my knees apart. Cheryl lay down in a similar position facing me, with our vulvas about a foot apart. Then she squirted a drop of lube on each end of the dildo and pressed one end against her opening. As she shimmied her hips toward me, half of the dildo slowly disappeared inside her pussy. When the other end pressed against my hole, I mimicked her movement until the plug was fully inserted inside our bodies with our vulvas mashed together.

"Are you *in* yet?" Cheryl joked, lifting her head off the floor and peering toward me.

"Judging by the feel of your wet pussy pressing against mine, I'd say so," I meowed.

"Shall we get started then?" she said.

"By all means," I purred.

As we both began rolling our hips together, I felt the dildo thrusting in and out of me as it plunged deeper and deeper inside my cunt. Although it wasn't vibrating yet and it didn't have the beneficial shape of some of the other curved vibrators, the feeling of Cheryl actively fucking me with the unicock and the sensation of her wet lips grinding against mine more than made up for the lack of other features.

Suddenly, she rolled over onto her side and straddled me with one leg under my ass and the other one over my tummy. As she humped me more aggressively, she began to grunt like a wild animal. I was enjoying the experience of being on the bottom for a change, but just as I began to feel the familiar feeling of another orgasm rising up within me, she turned over another ninety degrees until she was facing face-down on the carpet.

"Fuck me from behind, Jade," she groaned. "I want to feel your ass slapping against mine."

"Fuck yes!" I said, quickly rolling over so we were both facing down.

We pulled our knees forward and lifted ourselves up until we were resting on all-fours with our butt cheeks pressing against one another. Cheryl reached between her legs and pinched the middle of the dildo, and the snake suddenly began writhing inside our pussies as the ring between our legs flapped against our two clits.

"Oh God," I moaned as Cheryl began rocking her hips against me, slapping her ass against mine.

The simultaneous feeling of the gyrating dildo in my pussy with

Cheryl's ass grinding against mine and the vibrating ring trembling against my burning clit felt incredible.

"*Fuck*, Cheryl," I hissed. "I'm gonna cum. I'm gonna cum so hard all over your pretty ass. Come with me baby."

"I'm close," Cheryl growled. "Spray all over my wet hole. Let me feel you cum all over my burning cunt."

Whether it was Cheryl's sexy dirty talk or the sensation of being watched by all the other women around the room, I felt my orgasm suddenly wash over me as I began to shake uncontrollably against Cheryl's ass. My pussy clamped down hard on the flexible dildo as I felt the juices squirting out of my hole all over her opening.

"Yes, Jade!" she wailed. "Spray me with your cum. I'm coming baby! Fill up my hole as you cum inside me!"

As we both pawed the carpet like two cats in heat, I heard the sighs of other women around me and turned my head to see every one of them fucking themselves with one device or another as they watched us, their breasts trembling as they came in simultaneous union with Cheryl and me.

7

———

As the two of us lay spent and exhausted on the floor, I looked up at the other women peering at one another expectantly. It was obvious that they were ready to engage more actively with some of the others, and this seemed like the ideal time to open things up for broader participation. Cheryl and I looked at each other, thinking the same thing, and nodded.

"This seems like a good time for the rest of you to find a partner and try some interactive play," I said. "Feel free to grab whatever toy you can find and experiment away. It's always a lot more fun when you bring someone else into the mix, and there's a limitless degree of combinations you can create when you bring other partners into the equation. Grab a spot on the sofa, or use one of my private rooms, or join the rest of us on the floor. This party is a long way from being over!"

Almost immediately, all the other girls joined us on the floor, pairing up with new and old acquaintances, as they picked up various loose toys and rubbing them against each other's bodies. I peered over in Alana's direction and noticed that she was sitting by herself, looking at my naked body longingly. I turned to Cheryl, still joined at the hips with me on the floor, and she motioned for me to go to her. I pulled myself off my half of the dildo and Hannah quickly took my place, smiling at Cheryl as they pressed their hips together.

I was happy to see my friends hooking up and enjoying themselves so openly, but as I walked toward Alana crossing her legs shyly, I felt sorry for the one person in the group who still seemed hesitant to participate in the group fun.

"Haven't you been enjoying the party?" I said, taking a seat on the chair beside her.

"Yes, of course," Alana said, placing her arms shyly over her chest.

"I've noticed you participating at various times," I smiled. "But you seem reluctant to engage with the others. Are you feeling uncomfortable?"

"No—not really," she said. "It's just that no one else here...*interests* me."

I sensed what Alana was getting at, but I wanted to be sure before taking the next step.

"No one else meaning..."

"*You*, Jade," she said, peering into my eyes. "I've been watching you for so long, wanting to make love to you."

I slipped off my chair and kneeled in front of her, kissing her softly on her lips.

"I've been watching you from afar also, Alana," I said. "I've had many a sleepless night fantasizing about your beautiful figure, imagining myself touching and licking your naked body."

I lowered myself down the front of her body, nibbling the side of her neck and kissing the top of her chest. When I reached her firm breasts, I cupped each one in my hands and ran my tongue over her nipples in gentle circles. I could feel her nubs hardening in my mouth as I sucked on them gently. Alana tilted her head back and moaned, pressing her body toward me. As I moved in closer, she spread her legs further apart, and I could feel the heat emanating from her pussy.

Eager to feel her in my mouth, I continued lower until my face was level with her mound. I was a little surprised to find her so smooth and bare down there, and I looked up at her with a quizzical look.

"I shaved myself just for you," she said. "I didn't want anything coming between the two of us tonight."

I smiled up at her then rolled my cheeks against her soft pubis, flapping my eyelids with butterfly kisses against her skin as her thighs trembled in anticipation of my touch further below.

"Suck me, Jade," Alana whinnied, pressing her hips harder toward me. "I want to feel your lips on my most private parts. I've been dreaming about this for so long—"

Before she could finish her sentence, I lowered my face and encircled her flaming clit in my mouth, rolling my tongue over her pearl. Alana gasped and grabbed the back of my head, pulling me harder against her soaking vulva. I hummed in approval, alternating between flicking my tongue over her erect shaft and sucking her button deeply into my mouth. Her clit was larger than most, and I could feel her sex extend a full inch into my mouth as I sucked on her little cocklet.

Alana began rocking her hips wildly on her chair as she fucked my mouth shamelessly. Her groans grew progressively louder but just as I was sure she was about to come in my mouth, she suddenly pulled away and peered down at me with a possessed look on her face.

"I want to feel you inside me when I cum," she said. "Fuck me, Jade. Fuck me with one of Cheryl's sexy toys. I want to be your bitch."

I shook my head in shock, momentarily taken aback by Alana's newfound boldness. Whether this was simply her straight side wanting to get fucked in the manner she was accustomed to, or she was demonstrating her desire to adopt the femme persona in our new lesbian tryst, I didn't care. I just wanted to take her and consummate our long, lingering relationship as quickly as I could. My eyes darted along the floor to find something I could fuck her with, but seeing that all the other toys were in use by the other women engaged in heated affairs, I peered into Cheryl's case and noticed a strap-on dildo.

"Wait here, babe," I said. "I think I have just the thing."

I walked gingerly around all the writhing bodies on the floor and reached slowly into her case. Hannah and Cheryl were nearing the point of no return as they fucked each other wildly with the two-ended dildo, and they smiled at me devilishly as my breasts wobbled above their faces.

"Go fuck that girl," Hannah said. "Show her what it's like to experience a real orgasm."

I nodded at her then scampered back to Alana's chair where I found her already kneeling on the floor with her glistening ass pointed up toward me.

"Yes, Jade," she purred. "Fuck me with that big dildo. Let me feel your big cock deep inside me."

It didn't take more than a few seconds to wrap the belt around my waist and legs to secure the big phallus over my mound. It had a gentle downward curve and a thick head specifically intended for G-spot stimulation when used from behind. I noticed a couple of buttons on the front of the harness, but I was in too much of a hurry to feel Alana's pussy wrapped around my cock to figure out what they did. I reached between her legs to see if she needed any lubrication and she was slippery as a runny faucet. I pointed the tip of the dildo against her hole and wasted no time slamming it inside her cavern. If she wanted it rough, I thought, I was only too happy to oblige.

"Oh *fuck*!" Alana groaned. "That feels so good. Can you feel me squeezing you?"

I couldn't of course, because it was an artificial dildo. But I could feel the resistance of her tight pussy clamping against my faux cock as I pulled it out and slammed it back into her. The feeling of her ass cheeks slapping against my mound and my throbbing clit just amplified the feeling of fucking her like a man. I wondered what her husband would think if he knew what I was doing to his wife behind my closed curtains.

From her escalating moans and movements, I could tell that she was close to popping off, and I selfishly wanted to come with her. Maybe it was from me channeling the replacement of her husband or maybe it was just me desperately wanting to get off again. But either way, as sexy as it was to screw this little vixen with my artificial cock, I wasn't getting quite enough direct stimulation to get there with her.

I pulled out of her halfway for a moment and tapped a few of the buttons on the front of my harness. Suddenly, the dildo began throbbing with a deep rumble and another motor began vibrating against my nub under the harness.

"Holy shit," Alana hissed. "This thing is *way* better than my husband's cock. Whatever you're doing, it's driving me crazy. Fuck me harder, Jade. I'm getting close."

"So am I," I grunted, overwhelmed by the multiple sensations of fucking my neighbor from behind while simultaneously getting jilled on my clit. "Come with me baby. Let me feel you gushing all over my dick."

"Yes, Jade!" Alana cried. "Here it comes—I'm cumming!!"

Suddenly, I lost all sense of control as every ounce of my pent-up passion poured out of my body. As I began shuddering with intense contractions, I gushed my wetness out the sides of my harness down both sides of Alana's inner thighs. Feeling me cumming all over her, she wailed at the top of her lungs as her hips began shaking in spastic convulsions. I leaned over and squeezed her tits firmly with my hands as we both grunted in ecstatic union. When the two of us finished our long and intense climax and finally collapsed together on the floor, I noticed the rest of the girls lying beside us with silly grins on their faces.

This was one party none of us would soon forget.

VOLUME FOUR

MAID SERIVCE

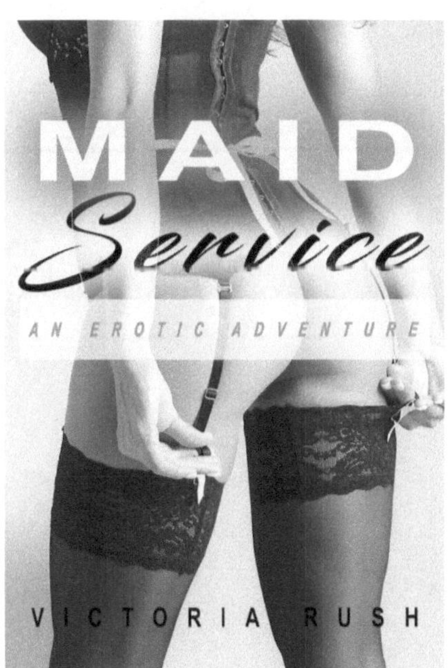

1

<hr>

It had been a long week on the road, and I was beginning to feel a bit antsy. I'd never really enjoyed business travel. The days were usually long, and my nights were often spent preparing for the following day's meetings. Granted, my clients took me out for a nice dinner afterwards, but those too were tiring, as I had to keep my game face on trying to land another hard-fought commission.

Being a freelance graphic designer was a tough gig, and I was always mindful of the need to coddle my buyer while not appearing to oversell my services. The idea of using these getaways for a quick hookup with a new acquaintance was out of the question. Not only was I usually too tired at the end of the day, but I had to keep a professional distance with my business associates.

I'd gotten up early to prepare for an important presentation later in the day, and after rubbing out a quick orgasm and having a shower, I sat down in front of my laptop at the small desk in my hotel room. But after reviewing a few slides of my PowerPoint deck, I paused and stared at the screen. This was the least fun part of my job, and I shifted the cursor over the address bar of my browser, preparing to type in the URL for my favorite lesbian website. I was still buzzing from my morning play time, and my panties were already wet thinking about watching some hot girls tribbing their pussies together. Just as I was about to take off my clothes and make myself more comfortable, I heard a gentle tap on my door.

"Housekeeping," a soft voice called.

Normally I'd ask the maid to return later in the day when I wasn't so busy. But I was caught unprepared and hastily pulled my jeans up before responding.

"Um–just a moment, please," I stammered.

I looked in the mirror at the front of the table and straightened my hair, trying to compose myself.

"Come in," I said, feeling my heartbeat returning to normal.

The maid opened the door and wedged her cart in the entrance, then hesitated when she saw me working at the table. She was younger and prettier than I expected, with dark brown eyes, soft caramel-colored skin, and puffy rosebud lips. I took a quick scan of her curvy figure and sat upright in my chair.

"Don't mind me," I said, feeling my pussy twitch unconsciously. "I'm just getting caught up on some work. Do you mind if I finish up while you clean the room?"

"Of course," she said. "I'll just be a few minutes."

She grabbed some fresh linens from her cart and disappeared into the bathroom. As I listened to her hanging up the towels and wiping down the counter, I suddenly remembered that I'd left my used vibrator next to the sink. Horrified, I glanced up and saw her pushing it to the side of the table while she peered up at me in the mirror. I blushed a deep shade of crimson and returned my gaze to my computer, pretending to tap away at the keyboard.

What the fuck, Jade, I muttered to myself, shaking my head in dismay. *Couldn't you have hidden the damn thing before you left the washroom?*

The maid seemed to take longer than usual to wipe down the surface as she rearranged my toiletries into a neat pile at the corner of the sink. I always felt a bit peeved whenever the housekeeping staff moved my personal effects, but today I was more put off than usual. Recognizing more movement out of the corner of my eye, I turned once again to see her leaning over and wiggling her ass as she finished wiping down the countertop.

She was wearing a one-piece black dress with a buttoned-up white collar and a short apron tied around her shapely hips. As she bent over and cleaned the vanity, I watched the muscles in the back of her legs flex while she swayed her hips in little circles. She caught my gaze once again in the bathroom mirror and smiled at me demurely.

Fuck me, I thought. *Are all the maids in this place this hot?*

I returned my attention to my computer and banged away at the keyboard as a jumble of random characters filled my slide. At this point, I had no idea what was appearing on my screen while I fantasied about kneeling between the girl's legs and slurping her pussy from behind. I could feel the wet spot beginning to grow in my panties, and I shifted uncomfortably on my chair, trying to distract attention from my aching clit.

When she emerged from the washroom, I turned toward her and noticed that she'd placed my purple Rabbit vibrator standing up on the side of the counter next to my toothbrush. The simulated penis head and protruding rabbit ears on the shaft stared out at me, mocking me for my absent-minded oversight.

Jesus Christ, I thought. *I wonder what she made of the unusual dildo. Had she even seen one of those things before?*

The thought of her touching my sex toy got me even more worked up as I imagined her pleasuring herself with the multi-functional device. Of course, I couldn't say anything, let alone acknowledge that she'd actually *touched* the object that had throbbed inside my pussy only a few minutes earlier.

As she strode toward my unmade bed, I was tempted to tell her to leave it as it was, since I knew it was hotel policy not to replace the linens until the next guest arrived. There wasn't really any need to make it up, since no one else would be seeing it for the remainder of the day and I'd just be climbing back into it in a matter of hours. But as I watched her glide around the side of the bed, I was so mesmerized watching her body in the mirror, I felt paralyzed.

As she leaned over the edge of the mattress, pulling the sheets toward the headboard, I saw her side profile for the first time. Even though her dress was buttoned all the way up the front of her chest, I could clearly see the outline of her breasts against the background of the stark white linens. Her tits were long and pointed, with wide separation between each peak, like she was wearing an old-fashioned corset underneath her tight uniform. With her light brown hair pulled back in a bun behind her head, I studied every curve and contour of her pretty face. Her cheekbones were high and round like a native American, but her cheeks were carved like a supermodel's. With her golden-brown skin and smoldering eyes, she looked like a cross between Jessica Alba and Jennifer Lopez.

Oh my God, I drooled, staring at her in my mirror. *How has this angel not already been swooped up by some handsome billionaire and whisked away to his private enclave? Was this her first week on the job and still too naive to know that with that body and those looks, she could write her own ticket?*

As she smoothed down the sheets and wrapped them around the base of the mattress, I leered at her tight ass, fantasizing about all the ways I'd like to fuck her. By now, my panties were so soaked, I'd formed a large wet patch in the crotch of my pants, and I squeezed my thighs together, trying to quiet my raging clit.

When the girl swept around the base of the bed directly behind me, I smelled her perfume, as a light breeze wafted over my shoulders. It smelled sweet and flowery, just like I imagined her to be. I couldn't make out the brand, but I resolved right then and there to go to the nearest department store at my earliest opportunity to find it for myself. Even if it didn't suit me personally, I longed to feel her scent on my body while I fantasied about rubbing our bodies together.

When she shifted over to the other side of the bed to repeat the sequence, I angled my head in the mirror to watch her ass in the reflection of the large picture window overlooking the street. As she leaned over, she swung one of her legs up to support herself while she propped up the pillows in the middle of my oversize bed, and I caught a glimpse of the back of her thighs and a small patch of white cloth between her legs.

Oh, I moaned out loud, imagining what she'd look like completely naked. I wanted this sexy vixen, and I wanted her *now*. But short of jumping on top of her and pinning her to my bed, I was completely at her mercy while I watched her go about her duties. Besides, the door was still ajar, and we'd have no privacy if either one of us had any amorous ideas.

She rearranged the room service menu and placed a fresh bottle of water at the side of the table next to me, then peered up at me in the mirror and smiled.

"Was there anything else you needed, Madam?" she asked.

I paused for a long moment as the words stuck in my throat.

I wanted to tell her how much I wanted to make a mess of her newly remade bed while I wrapped my legs around her and plunged my tongue down her throat, but I shook my head and sighed.

"No," I said. "Thank you for everything. I'm good to go."

She nodded at me, then pushed her housekeeping cart over the threshold, softly closing the door behind her.

Good to go? I thought to myself. *What a lightweight you are, Jade. If you had any guts, you'd have taken her in your arms and kissed her like a proper lady.* After all, she'd given me plenty of clues that she was just as interested in me as I was with her.

As soon as I heard her move her cart to the next room and knock on the adjacent door, I leapt to my feet and grabbed my Rabbit vibrator off the bathroom countertop. Then I tore off my clothes and kneeled on my bed, facing the desk mirror. As I plunged the phallus deep into my dripping pussy and turned the setting to max, I dreamed it was the pretty maid who was staring back at me.

I still have three days to get you into my bed, I murmured. *One way or the other, I'll have you before this week is over.*

2

———

It had been a long week on the road, and I was beginning to feel a bit antsy. I'd never really enjoyed business travel. The days were usually long, and my nights were often spent preparing for the following day's meetings. Granted, my clients took me out for a nice dinner afterwards, but those too were tiring, as I had to keep my game face on trying to land another hard-fought commission.

Being a freelance graphic designer was a tough gig, and I was always mindful of the need to coddle my buyer while not appearing to oversell my services. The idea of using these getaways for a quick hookup with a new acquaintance was out of the question. Not only was I usually too tired at the end of the day, but I had to keep a professional distance with my business associates.

I'd gotten up early to prepare for an important presentation later in the day, and after rubbing out a quick orgasm and having a shower, I sat down in front of my laptop at the small desk in my hotel room. But after reviewing a few slides of my PowerPoint deck, I paused and stared at the screen. This was the least fun part of my job, and I shifted the cursor over the address bar of my browser, preparing to type in the URL for my favorite lesbian website. I was still buzzing from my morning play time, and my panties were already wet thinking about watching some hot girls tribbing their pussies together. Just as I was about to take off my clothes and make myself more comfortable, I heard a gentle tap on my door.

"Housekeeping," a soft voice called.

Normally I'd ask the maid to return later in the day when I wasn't so busy. But I was caught unprepared and hastily pulled my jeans up before responding.

"Um–just a moment, please," I stammered.

I looked in the mirror at the front of the table and straightened my hair, trying to compose myself.

"Come in," I said, feeling my heartbeat returning to normal.

The maid opened the door and wedged her cart in the entrance, then hesitated when she saw me working at the table. She was younger and prettier than I expected, with dark brown eyes, soft caramel-colored skin, and puffy rosebud lips. I took a quick scan of her curvy figure and sat upright in my chair.

"Don't mind me," I said, feeling my pussy twitch unconsciously. "I'm just getting caught up on some work. Do you mind if I finish up while you clean the room?"

"Of course," she said. "I'll just be a few minutes."

She grabbed some fresh linens from her cart and disappeared into the bathroom. As I listened to her hanging up the towels and wiping down the counter, I suddenly remembered that I'd left my used vibrator next to the sink. Horrified, I glanced up and saw her pushing it to the side of the table while she peered up at me in the mirror. I blushed a deep shade of crimson and returned my gaze to my computer, pretending to tap away at the keyboard.

What the fuck, Jade, I muttered to myself, shaking my head in dismay. *Couldn't you have hidden the damn thing before you left the washroom?*

The maid seemed to take longer than usual to wipe down the surface as she rearranged my toiletries into a neat pile at the corner of the sink. I always felt a bit peeved whenever the housekeeping staff moved my personal effects, but today I was more put off than usual. Recognizing more movement out of the corner of my eye, I turned once again to see her leaning over and wiggling her ass as she finished wiping down the countertop.

She was wearing a one-piece black dress with a buttoned-up white collar and a short apron tied around her shapely hips. As she bent over and cleaned the vanity, I watched the muscles in the back of her legs flex while she swayed her hips in little circles. She caught my gaze once again in the bathroom mirror and smiled at me demurely.

Fuck me, I thought. *Are all the maids in this place this hot?*

I returned my attention to my computer and banged away at the keyboard as a jumble of random characters filled my slide. At this point, I had no idea what was appearing on my screen while I fantasied about kneeling between the girl's legs and slurping her pussy from behind. I could feel the wet spot beginning to grow in my panties, and I shifted uncomfortably on my chair, trying to distract attention from my aching clit.

When she emerged from the washroom, I turned toward her and noticed that she'd placed my purple Rabbit vibrator standing up on the side of the counter next to my toothbrush. The simulated penis head and protruding rabbit ears on the shaft stared out at me, mocking me for my absent-minded oversight.

Jesus Christ, I thought. *I wonder what she made of the unusual dildo. Had she even seen one of those things before?*

The thought of her touching my sex toy got me even more worked up as I imagined her pleasuring herself with the multi-functional device. Of course, I couldn't say anything, let alone acknowledge that she'd actually *touched* the object that had throbbed inside my pussy only a few minutes earlier.

As she strode toward my unmade bed, I was tempted to tell her to leave it as it was, since I knew it was hotel policy not to replace the linens until the next guest arrived. There wasn't really any need to make it up, since no one else would be seeing it for the remainder of the day and I'd just be climbing back into it in a matter of hours. But as I watched her glide around the side of the bed, I was so mesmerized watching her body in the mirror, I felt paralyzed.

As she leaned over the edge of the mattress, pulling the sheets toward the headboard, I saw her side profile for the first time. Even though her dress was buttoned all the way up the front of her chest, I could clearly see the outline of her breasts against the background of the stark white linens. Her tits were long and pointed, with wide separation between each peak, like she was wearing an old-fashioned corset underneath her tight uniform. With her light brown hair pulled back in a bun behind her head, I studied every curve and contour of her pretty face. Her cheekbones were high and round like a native American, but her cheeks were carved like a supermodel's. With her golden-brown skin and smoldering eyes, she looked like a cross between Jessica Alba and Jennifer Lopez.

Oh my God, I drooled, staring at her in my mirror. *How has this angel not already been swooped up by some handsome billionaire and whisked away to his private enclave? Was this her first week on the job and still too naive to know that with that body and those looks, she could write her own ticket?*

As she smoothed down the sheets and wrapped them around the base of the mattress, I leered at her tight ass, fantasizing about all the ways I'd like to fuck her. By now, my panties were so soaked, I'd formed a large wet patch in the crotch of my pants, and I squeezed my thighs together, trying to quiet my raging clit.

When the girl swept around the base of the bed directly behind me, I smelled her perfume, as a light breeze wafted over my shoulders. It smelled sweet and flowery, just like I imagined her to be. I couldn't make out the brand, but I resolved right then and there to go to the nearest department store at my earliest opportunity to find it for myself. Even if it didn't suit me personally, I longed to feel her scent on my body while I fantasied about rubbing our bodies together.

When she shifted over to the other side of the bed to repeat the sequence, I angled my head in the mirror to watch her ass in the reflection of the large picture window overlooking the street. As she leaned over, she swung one of her legs up to support herself while she propped up the pillows in the middle of my oversize bed, and I caught a glimpse of the back of her thighs and a small patch of white cloth between her legs.

Oh, I moaned out loud, imagining what she'd look like completely naked. I wanted this sexy vixen, and I wanted her *now*. But short of jumping on top of her and pinning her to my bed, I was completely at her mercy while I watched her go about her duties. Besides, the door was still ajar, and we'd have no privacy if either one of us had any amorous ideas.

She rearranged the room service menu and placed a fresh bottle of water at the side of the table next to me, then peered up at me in the mirror and smiled.

"Was there anything else you needed, Madam?" she asked.

I paused for a long moment as the words stuck in my throat.

I wanted to tell her how much I wanted to make a mess of her newly remade bed while I wrapped my legs around her and plunged my tongue down her throat, but I shook my head and sighed.

"No," I said. "Thank you for everything. I'm good to go."

She nodded at me, then pushed her housekeeping cart over the threshold, softly closing the door behind her.

Good to go? I thought to myself. *What a lightweight you are, Jade. If you had any guts, you'd have taken her in your arms and kissed her like a proper lady.* After all, she'd given me plenty of clues that she was just as interested in me as I was with her.

As soon as I heard her move her cart to the next room and knock on the adjacent door, I leapt to my feet and grabbed my Rabbit vibrator off the bathroom countertop. Then I tore off my clothes and kneeled on my bed, facing the desk mirror. As I plunged the phallus deep into my dripping pussy and turned the setting to max, I dreamed it was the pretty maid who was staring back at me.

I still have three days to get you into my bed, I murmured. *One way or the other, I'll have you before this week is over.*

3

———————

I was so fixated fantasizing about the pretty maid for the rest of the morning, I was late for my scheduled meeting with my client. When I got to the office, I could barely concentrate on my presentation, flashing back and forth between her exquisite ass and her Gina Lollobrigida tits. Everybody else in my sphere of influence suddenly seemed so dull and boring. When my buyer invited me for dinner that evening, I reluctantly agreed, knowing I'd have an even harder time concentrating as I dreamt about slipping back under my covers, smelling her intoxicating scent.

When I returned to my hotel room, I lifted the pillow to my face and inhaled her heavenly aroma. For a moment, I contemplated rubbing out another quick one, but I only had a half hour to change my clothes and freshen up. As I leaned over the sink to reapply my mascara and straighten my lipstick, I glanced at my Rabbit vibrator still lying on the counter. Thinking back to how the maid had nonchalantly picked it up and placed it upright next to the sink made my pussy flutter in unconscious spasms.

Fuck it, I huffed, grabbing the dildo and pulling my panties down below my knees. I've still got a few minutes, and nobody will be any the wiser if I have a little fun before heading out to another boring client dinner.

Just as I was about to thrust the oscillating tip into my sopping tunnel, I heard another soft tap on my door.

"Turndown service," a familiar voice called.

Holy shit! I gushed. *Could it be the same girl? How could I be this lucky to see her again so soon?*

"Come in," I said, thrusting my vibrator into the side pocket of the hotel robe hanging on the back of the bathroom door.

When the girl opened the door and saw me in the bathroom, I peered back at her and smiled.

"I'm just getting ready to go out," I said. "Feel free to do your thing while I finish up."

"No worries," the maid said, leaving her cart outside the door and walking toward the center of my room.

I'd always wondered what maids did during turndown service, since I'd been away from my room or too busy to be bothered when they called. But this time, I was intrigued for a number of reasons, and after composing myself in the mirror, I walked out into the room pretending to collect my things.

"I always seem to be getting in your way," I said, watching her collect the throw cushions at my headboard and neatly arranging them on the bench at the base of the bed.

"Not at all," the girl said, laying my pillows down flat on the mattress.

As she worked quietly, I peered at her gorgeous ass, perfectly framed by the white apron tied around her waist.

"I always *wondered* what you guys did during turndown service," I said, looking for an excuse to keep watching her.

She turned her head and caught me staring at her skirt.

"It's mostly just getting the bed ready for you to turn into later this evening," she smiled. "And straightening up a few things like the breakfast menu and the minibar."

I smiled, imagining she was turning *me* over instead, while she ran her hands all over my body.

"I thought it might be something a little more exotic," I mused.

"Oh?" she said. "Was there something else you wanted?"

"Um..." I hesitated for a long moment. Then I chickened out and shook my head.

"No," I said, watching her fold the sheets down into a neat triangle at the side of the bed. "You're doing everything perfectly."

"Thank you," the girl nodded, peering up at me. "I'm still kind of new to this, so any suggestions are most welcome."

"I bet you find some rooms are a little more–*unkempt*–than others," I said, reflecting back on how she'd stumbled upon my vibrator resting on the bathroom counter earlier in the day.

"Some guests are a little neater than others, to be sure," she said, taking a little extra time to plump the pillows at the head of the bed.

"But yours is easier than most," she smiled, lowering her gaze to the cleavage showing in my partially unbuttoned silk blouse.

"Do people sometimes leave things behind?" I said, hoping to steer the conversation in a new direction.

"Oh yes," she said. "Everything you can imagine. Laptops, belts, pieces of clothing–"

"And *other* personal effects?" I smiled.

"Sometimes," she blushed. "But we store everything in the lost and found in case customers want to reclaim them."

"And if they don't?" I said. "Do the housekeeping staff get to keep them as the spoils of their work?"

She placed the breakfast menu on my side table with a fresh bottle of water.

"Not usually. The hotel tries to contact them, and if we don't hear back after a certain period of time, we usually throw it out."

"That must be frustrating," I said. "I once accidentally left an expensive coat in an overhead storage bin on an airplane and never had it returned."

"They couldn't find it?" the girl enquired.

"Apparently not," I said. "I always wondered if whoever cleans the plane simply didn't report it and kept it for themselves."

"That must have been infuriating," the maid said, heading toward the bathroom to check on my supplies.

"Not so much infuriating as embarrassing," I said. "It was the *personal* effects I left in my pocket that bothered me the most."

"Yes, I can imagine," she said, returning to the side of my bed carrying my robe and a pair of terrycloth slippers. "Was it something valuable?"

"Not in monetary terms," I said, widening my eyes as she laid the robe on the edge of the mattress and placed the slippers at the side of the bed. "Just little trinkets I carry with me to keep me amused on long flights."

She felt the lump in the pocket of my robe and reached in to extract my vibrator.

"Like *this* one?" she smiled, placing it upright on the night table beside the bed. "I don't think you'll want this falling into the wrong hands."

"It depends *whose* hands it is," I smiled at her with a raised eyebrow.

The girl paused for a long moment, as we ran our eyes over one another's bodies.

"Do you mind if I ask how it works?" she asked. "I've never seen anything quite like it before."

"*Oh my God*," I said. "You haven't seen the famous Sex in the City episode where Miranda introduces her newfound sex toy to her best friends?"

"No..."

"*Come*," I said excitedly. "Scooch down next to me while I show you what this amazing device can do."

I sat down on the edge of the bed and held out my hand, pulling her down next to me. Then I grabbed the dildo off the nightstand and tapped a button on the base of the unit. I handed the shaking device to the girl, and she wrapped her hand around the shaft.

"Okay..." she said, shaking her head. "That's not so different from most vibrators."

So she has used vibrators before, I said to myself.

"That's only one of *many* ways it can stimulate you," I smiled.

I tapped another button and suddenly the chrome beads embedded inside the translucent shaft began rotating in circles.

The girl's eyes widened as she felt the beads rubbing against her palm, and she took her hand away to inspect the whirring object.

"And get *this*," I said, pressing a knob at the base of the unit.

Suddenly, the head of the penis-shaped phallus began twisting from side-to-side like a possessed wobble-head doll.

"*Holy crap*," the girl said, shifting her weight unsteadily on the bed.

"You've never had your G-spot stimulated in quite the same way until you've tried this baby," I smirked.

"Is *this* the thing you left in your coat pocket on the airplane?" she gasped.

"No, I've got a smaller and quieter device I use to keep myself amused on airplanes. Maybe I'll show you that another day. But there's one *other* feature I wanted to show you on this special toy."

I tapped another button on the base of the unit and suddenly the silicone rabbit ears extending from the side of the shaft began fluttering rapidly.

"These little fingers stimulate your clitoris while all that other action is going on inside."

"No *way*," the girl said, holding her fingers over the flapping ears.

"Do you want to give it a try?" I smiled.

"Right *here*?!" she said. "What about the other guests–"

"It won't take long, *believe* me," I said, squeezing her thigh gently. "With this multi-talented toy, you'll be satisfied in a matter of seconds."

"I don't know..." the girl hesitated, peering toward the closed door. "I don't want to get into any trouble..."

"I won't tell if you don't," I said, thrilled that she was showing newfound interest in my toy. "Here–why don't *I* show you first?"

I pulled off my clothes and threw them on the adjacent bed, then kicked off my heels and sat back against the headboard, spreading my legs.

"Oh my God..." the girl panted, peering down at my glistening labia.

Maybe this business trip isn't going to be quite so boring after all, I smiled to myself.

4

———

"Watch and enjoy, sweetheart," I said, pointing the tip of the rotating dildo toward my opening. "*Mmm*," I moaned as it sank deeper into my tunnel.

When I'd pressed the vibrator as far as I could into my hole, I tapped the button activating the throbbing head and pulled my knees up, rocking my hips in delight. The pretty girl sat frozen on the bed, staring between my legs while I rammed the artificial cock in and out of my slurping pussy.

"You like what you see?" I said, feeling my passion rapidly rising with her watching me only inches away. "Now for the coup de grâce."

I tapped the button to activate the rabbit ears, and the flaps began buzzing against my inflamed gland. I threw my head back against the headboard and pulled the dildo harder against my snatch.

"I'm going to cum, baby," I panted, feeling the wall of pleasure about to overtake me. "Tell me your name."

"Luna," she purred, shifting closer to me on the bed.

"I'm *cumming*, Luna," I groaned as she met my gaze, yawning her mouth open in sympathy with me.

She leaned in and sucked my erect nipples into her mouth, and I whined in ecstasy from the combination of sensations that were attacking my body.

"*Fuck yes!*" I squealed, as my whole body shook like I was having an epileptic seizure. "Suck my tits baby."

I couldn't believe this heavenly angel was actually touching me while I had one of the most powerful orgasms of my life. I hadn't come so hard and so fast in a long time, but there was something incredibly hot about this sweet girl watching me while I pleasured myself.

When I finally stopped shaking, I took the dildo out of my pussy and kissed Luna on the lips. She nibbled my upper lip and I thrust my tongue into her, pulling the back of her head toward me. She moaned in my mouth, and I reached out to grasp her pointy tits, squeezing them firmly.

"Now that we've gotten to know each other a little better, my name's Jade," I smiled, unbuttoning the top of her dress. "Let's get you out of these clothes."

"Okay," she said, peering toward the door uncertainly. "But I can't take too long. My supervisor will be wondering what's holding things up..."

"I won't keep you long," I said. "Maybe we can find some more quiet time later in the evening. Don't you want to give this a try before you go?" I lifted the vibrator off the bed and flipped my legs over the side of the mattress. "Just give me a sec to wash it off first–"

"No," Luna said, pulling the Rabbit out of my hands. "I'll enjoy it more this way. It's already lubed up and ready to go."

She stood up and untied her apron, then pulled her dress down over her hips and placed it neatly on the opposite bed. Then she reached behind her back and unclasped her bra, freeing her unusually shaped tits. She had large brown areolas and thick pointy nipples, giving her boobs in the appearance of butternut squash.

Very tasty butternut squash.

"Oh my God, Luna," I said, shifting over to give her room to sit on the mattress next to me. "Come here so I can suck on those melons. You have the most delicious breasts I've ever seen."

Luna sat down next to me, and I cupped her gourds in my palms, marveling at how buoyant they were given their pointy shape.

"Do you have any idea how beautiful you are?" I said, peering into her eyes.

"My mother tells me every day," she laughed.

"I meant with other *boys and girls* your age. Surely you must notice the way they look at you."

"I guess so," she said. "I always thought it was just because I'm slightly more *curvy* than the other girls."

"You're exceptional in *so* many other ways," I said, turning her chin toward me as I kissed her gently on the lips. "Have you ever been with another lover before?"

"Just some heavy petting with the boys at school. I've never been with another woman like this before..."

I pushed the Rabbit vibrator toward the side of the bed and pinched her nipples gently between my fingers.

"Let me show you what it's like to be touched by a woman. I think you'll find you don't always need *boy* parts to be satisfied."

"But what about the Rabbit toy?" she said, peering at my glistening vibrator lying on the bed.

"There'll be plenty of time for that another time. I'm staying at the hotel for a few more days. Now lie down while I worship your body."

I pulled the corner of the sheets toward the far end of the bed, and Luna lay down flat on the mattress. Then I pulled off her panties and lay next to her while we rubbed our bodies together softly. When she felt my breasts pressing up against her, she moaned softly and I kissed her, rolling my tongue around the inside of her mouth.

"Jade," she purred. "I love the feel of your body next to me. I've wanted you to touch me from the moment I saw you working at the desk."

"Oh *really*?" I said, pulling back in surprise. "You little tease. And here I thought you were ignoring me the whole time."

"How could I ignore you after smelling your scent on the vibrator you left on the counter? And I saw the way you were looking at me–"

"Were you bending over and shaking your ass more than usual to attract my attention?"

"Maybe..." she said, nuzzling her nose into the side of my cheek.

I smiled as I sucked on her puffy lips.

"Do you know what I've been fantasizing about all day long since I saw you?" I said.

"Showing me how to use your special vibrator?" she said.

"No," I purred. "Ever since I saw you leaning over the bathroom counter, I've been dreaming about licking your sweet pussy."

"I was thinking the same thing when I saw you staring at me."

"Did it make you *wet* when you thought about my face between your legs?"

"Mmm-hmm," Luna nodded.

"Spread your legs for me, baby. Let me feel what I've been dreaming about these last few hours."

Luna fanned her legs halfway apart, and I lifted myself up to position myself in her crevasse.

"God," I grunted, kissing my way up the inside of her thighs. "You smell exquisite. What *is* that perfume you're wearing, anyway?"

"Black Opium, by Yves Saint Laurent," she said.

"How perfect," I purred, peering at her dark labia framed by the thick patch of black hair resting on top of her pubis. "Let me smell your flower."

I pulled myself closer to her opening, then breathed in her perfume through my nostrils.

"You could attract any manner of pollinator with that heavenly scent," I said. "I feel lucky to be the first one to kiss you here."

"Yes," Luna panted, lifting her pelvis off the mattress. "Lick my pussy. Taste my nectar."

Normally, I would have teased her a little longer to build up her excitement, but I didn't need any further invitation. I lowered my head and enveloped her glistening jewel in my mouth, feeling her pubic hair brushing against my forehead. She tasted as sweet as honey, and I paused for a long moment, sucking her juices into my mouth. Luna groaned and pressed her mound harder against my face, and I extended my tongue, caressing the top of her lips.

"Yes, Jade," Luca purred. "Suck my rose. Spread me open like a blossoming flower."

"Mmm," I murmured, getting increasingly turned on by the botanic metaphor. I guessed there was a lot more to this intriguing maid than just a pretty face, and I was looking forward to learning about her other interests and passions. But right now, there was only one thing on my mind. Taking her cue, I lowered my head and pressed my tongue slowly into her cavity. Luna groaned and placed her hands behind my head, pulling me harder against her vulva.

"*Fuck yes*," she grunted, gripping my hair between her fists. "Fuck my pussy with your tongue, Jade. I want to cum all over your face."

I was taken aback by her sudden raunchy turn, but her dirty language just got me more worked up as I felt my juices making a giant wet spot on the mattress between my legs. I grabbed the side of her thighs and pressed my tongue as deep into her as I could, then swirled it around in circles, tasting her syrup.

As she began to rock her hips against my face and grip my hair ever tighter, my roots started to sting, but I was so turned on by her mounting passion, I paid no attention. As she began to thrash her hips wildly against my face, I ground my own pelvis against the mattress, imagining I was fucking her with my cunny instead of my face.

Suddenly, she arched her hips off the mattress and wailed out loud as I watched her tits shaking like two melons in a hurricane. Her giant areolas stared back at me with their flaring nipples as I sucked her juices out of her twitching pussy. Luna held me tight against her vulva for many long seconds as her body twisted and convulsed against my dripping face. When she finally stopped cumming, she released her grip on my hair and flopped back against the pillows propped up against the headboard.

"Jesus, girl," I said, peering up between her legs. "You don't hold back, do you?"

"I guess I've been saving up imagining what this would feel like," she said. "Sorry if I got a little carried away. Did I hurt you?"

"Only in the best possible way," I smiled. "That might have been the sexiest thing I've ever experienced."

Luna turned her wrist to look at her watch.

"I've got to get back to work before I get into trouble. Will you have some more time for us to get back together between your business meetings?"

"Are you *kidding* me?" I said, feeling my juices dribbling down the inside of my thighs. "Screw my client. *You're* my new project for the rest of the week."

I arrived at my dinner appointment twenty minutes late, using the feeble excuse of a family emergency. But my buyer must have wondered just what kind of 'emergency' had put such severe knots in my hair and rumpled my clothing so thoroughly. But I hardly cared, reflecting back on the memory of Luna's hips quivering over my face. For the rest of the dinner, I barely heard a thing he said, as I nibbled on the red peppers in my stir-fry and swirled the red wine around my mouth, remembering her exquisite taste.

When I got back to my hotel room, I propped myself up against the bed's headboard and watched myself in the desk mirror while I fucked myself with my vibrator, imagining her looking back at me. I slept like a baby that night, then got up early to have a long shower in the morning. I wanted to be as fresh as possible when Luna returned later that morning to do my room. I kept myself busy fantasizing about all the things I wanted to do with her as I introduced her to the joys of lesbian lovemaking. But when the tap finally arrived on my door, it was a different-sounding tone that greeted me.

Hiding my vibrator under the pillow fold in the adjacent bedspread, I opened the door to see an older, frumpy-looking maid. I motioned her into my room, then collected my belongings in preparation for heading to the office. But as I watched her go about her duties, I couldn't help asking about Luna.

"What happened to the girl who cleaned my room yesterday?" I asked.

"We're assigned different rooms every day, so she's probably busy cleaning another floor. Was there something special you needed?"

"No," I said, slumping my shoulders. "I just wanted to give her an extra tip for the special housekeeping services she provided yesterday."

"You can leave it in an envelope on your pillow when you check-out of your room. I'll mention it to her, so she remembers to pick it up."

I wasn't sure if she was telling me the full truth, but I was far more concerned that I'd embarrassed Luna or somehow scared her from returning to my room. Had I come on too strong during our first encounter? Had I misread the signals that she seemed just as interested in me as I was with her? Had her manager admonished her for taking too long to finish my room?

For the rest of the day, I had a hard time concentrating on my client presentations, worrying that I'd lost my chance to reconnect with the sweet Latina beauty. I canceled my dinner plans hoping she'd return for my turndown service that evening, while flipping through the channels on my in-room TV to keep myself distracted. When I heard a soft tap on my door, I practically leapt off my bed, feeling my heart racing in excitement. I tiptoed to the door and peered through the peephole. I was delighted to see Luna standing there with another pretty girl about her same age, both dressed in casual clothes.

I swung open the door and peered at her inquisitively.

"I wasn't sure if I was going to see you again," I said, pinching my eyebrows in dismay.

"Sorry," Luna said, turning her head both ways to glance down the empty hallway. "It was my day off today, and I didn't want any of the other hotel staff seeing me entering your room. We're not supposed to mingle with the guests."

"Of course," I said, looking at her pretty companion. "Did you have any special plans? Would you like to go out for some drinks?"

"This is my friend Gabriella," Luna said. "She works with me at the hotel. Do you mind if I bring her along?"

"Of course not," I said, smiling at the other girl. "I just need a moment to freshen up before heading out. Would you like to come in while I get ready?"

"Sure," Luna said.

I stuck my head out the door to make sure it was clear, then I ushered the two girls into my room.

"I was afraid I might have scared you away after we met yesterday. The new maid wasn't entirely sure where you were."

"I'm sorry..." Luna hesitated. "I didn't have your number and I–"

I noticed the girls shifting their weight awkwardly in the narrow walkway next to my bathroom and I motioned them toward the side of my bed.

"Would you like to make yourselves comfortable while I straighten myself up?"

"Yes, thank you."

I went into the washroom to put on some lipstick and leaned over the sink, trying to see their reflection in the mirror. I had no idea why she'd decided to bring a friend, but my pussy twitched wondering if they might be lovers.

"I didn't catch your friend's name," I called from the bathroom.

"Gabriella," Luna said. "We started around the same time."

"At the hotel? What do you do, Gabriella?"

"I'm a waitress in the downstairs restaurant," she replied.

"You're both so pretty," I said. "I can only imagine how many times you get propositioned by lonely middle-aged travelers."

"It's not so bad," Gabriella said. "As long as we keep a healthy distance and don't flirt too much, we manage to stay out of trouble."

I smiled, remembering how easy it was to lure Luna into my bed.

"Have you known each other very long?" I said, fishing for more details about their personal relationship.

"Just a few months," Luna said. "We kind of hit it off right away."

I was intrigued why Luna would bring her friend to our second date, knowing how sexually charged it was likely to be. As I stepped out of the lavatory brushing my hair, I caught them inspecting my Rabbit vibrator as they giggled quietly between them. I guessed that they'd seen it sticking out from under the covers, and Luna must have been describing its various features. When she tried to stuff it back under the pillow, I held up my hand.

"Don't put it away on *my* account," I smiled. "Have you ever seen one of those before, Gabriella?"

"I Googled it after Luna told me about it," she said. "I've just seen what it looks like on their website."

"It's hard to appreciate it from a *picture*," I said, pulling it back out from under the covers and sitting down on the bed next to Gabriella. "Here, why don't you press some of the buttons and see for yourself."

I handed the purple dildo to her, and she fumbled with it awkwardly.

"Press the little button on the left-hand side of the controller," I said.

Gabriella tapped it, and the chrome beads began whirring in circles around the middle of the shaft. She jumped in surprise and looked up at me inquisitively.

"I bet you've never seen a boy's cock do *that* before," I smiled.

"Um, no..." she said, blushing softly.

"Try *this* one," I said, pointing to the button just below it.

When she tapped it, the penis-shaped head of the dildo began twisting like a spinning top and she almost dropped it in her lap.

"I *know*," I nodded. "If only *every* man could be equipped that way."

"What are these strange things on the side?" she said, pointing to the flexible rabbit ears.

"That's what *really* makes this special," I grinned, suspecting that Luna had already described the unique features of my vibrator in meticulous detail. I tapped the button on the bottom of the device, and the rabbit ears began flapping rapidly. "These two little fingers stimulate your clitoris while the rest of the vibrator is turning around inside you."

I peered up at Gabriella, then smiled at Luna.

"But you already *knew* that, didn't you? I'm sure Luna's already given you a full accounting of its various functions. You didn't just come here for a few *drinks*, did you?"

"Um..." Luna hesitated, peering over at her friend.

"It's okay," I said, taking the vibrator out of her hands and placing it on the nightstand next to my bed. "I'm glad you brought a friend. There's *so* many more ways we can enjoy this together."

I stood up and took off my clothes, throwing the pieces on the bed next to them, then pulled down the covers on the adjacent bed.

"You never know when double beds might come in handy on a business trip," I grinned.

While I stood in front of the two girls completely naked, they ran their eyes over my figure, lingering especially long at my glistening, hairless mound. Then I held out my hand to Gabriella and motioned for her to join me on the opposite bed.

"Come," I said. "Something tells me this isn't the first time you girls have experimented with sex toys. Let me show you how the *three* of us can make this a little more fun."

I lifted Gabriella off the bed, then pulled her turtleneck over her head and slowly unclasped her bra. Her breasts were smaller than Luna's, but rounder and firmer, with pink areolas and small button-shaped nipples. I cupped them gently, then leaned in to give her a wet kiss.

"You're beautiful, Gabriella," I gushed. "I can see why the two of you came together so quickly. I haven't seen such a pretty pair in a long time."

I peered down at her tight jeans, admiring the youthful contour of her hips.

"Do you need help getting out of those pants?"

"Yes please," she said as I watched her nipples contract and harden in excitement.

I reached down and unclasped the button at the top of her waistband, then lowered the zipper and pulled her jeans down to the floor as she kicked them off to the side. Then I kneeled down between her thighs and pulled her panties down to the floor, and she stepped out of them. Her bush was trimmed more neatly than Luna's, with a tawny amber color, and I leaned in to kiss it while I reached around and cupped her buttocks gently. Her ass quivered as I lowered my mouth to her moist slit, and she gasped when I circled her nub with my lips.

"Mmm," I moaned, as she pressed her mound harder into my face.

I peered out of the side of my eyes at Luna still sitting on the edge of the other bed, noticing her hand moving gently in her lap. The thought of her watching me while I ate out her best friend thrilled me, and I began to roll my hips unconsciously as I licked and teased Gabriella's burning clit.

"Uhnn," she grunted, spreading her legs further apart and angling her hips until she was standing directly over top of me. I squeezed her cheeks while her buttocks clenched together, and from the pace of her breathing I knew it wouldn't be long before she reached the peak of her pleasure.

I tilted my head up and watched her little boobs bouncing on her chest as she ran her fingers through my hair. She wasn't as aggressive as Luna had been holding me while I sucked her pussy, and I guessed that she was the submissive one in the relationship.

"Oh *God*," Gabriella suddenly moaned as she slumped over me, jerking her body in spastic movements.

I could tell from the intensity of her rocking motion that she was cumming on my face, and I held her tightly until she stopped moving. I pulled my head back and peered over at Luna, who had her knees spread wide apart and was rubbing her hand vigorously over a large stain in the crotch of her jeans.

"I think somebody *else* is missing out on all the fun," I said, shifting over and pulling her pants down over her curvy hips.

This time she'd chosen to go pantyless, and I looked up at her with a mischievous smile.

"Were you in a hurry to get started tonight?" I grinned.

"Going bare just reminded me of what it felt like to have you next to me," she smiled. "I didn't want anything else getting in the way."

I pulled her off the bed and ripped off her T-shirt, thrilled to see her oval-shaped melons bouncing freely on her chest.

"*Gawd*, how I've fantasized about these since I last saw you," I panted, pulling her toward me, mashing our bodies together. "But first, I had something different in mind."

I yanked the opposite bedspread all the way down toward the baseboard and instructed the two girls to kneel on the mattress, facing one another.

"I want to watch you enjoy my special vibrator together."

I handed the dildo to Gabriella and smiled.

"Why don't you place the long end inside, then press your bodies together so you can *both* enjoy the vibrating rabbit ears?"

Gabriella looked at Luna, and her friend nodded back at her.

"Knock yourselves out while I make myself more comfortable," I smiled.

I leaned back on my mattress and began circling my clit while I watched the two girls rubbing their bodies together. Gabriella tapped the buttons on the base of the unit and slowly inserted the oscillating device into her hole. She gasped in surprise at the unusual sensation, and Luna wrapped her arms around her shoulders, pulling their bodies together. As Gabriella began to thrust the humming vibrator in and out of her pussy, Luna pressed her mound against her girl-friend, purring in delight.

"Press the knob on the bottom now," I said to Gabriella, inserting two fingers into my slit.

Gabriella peered over at me, and her eyes widened as she watched me finger-fucking myself with my knees spread wide apart. She reached behind her ass and flexed her finger, and I heard a loud buzzing sound emanating from between their legs. The two girls groaned in pleasure as they felt the rabbit ears flapping against their joined clits, then they pressed their faces together, tonguing each other wildly. The image of the two sexy girls rubbing their bodies together as the big dildo whirled, twisted, and buzzed between both of their legs was surreal.

"*Fuck* yes," I hissed, ramming my fingers harder into my cunt. "Rub your tits and cunnies together while I watch you come."

"Mmm," Luna moaned, placing her hands over Gabriella's buttocks. "Come with me, Gabby," she said. "I can feel the rabbit ears touching both of our clits."

"Yes," Gabby whinnied, reaching around to grab Luna's ass at the same time. "I'm cumming, Lou. Oh *God*, I'm *cumming*!"

The two girls tilted their heads back and wailed in unison as their bodies began to quiver and tremble in simultaneous orgasm. I'd been so focused on watching them rubbing their bodies together that I'd barely paid any attention to what *I* was feeling, but the sight of them cumming together with my favorite vibrator purring between their legs quickly put me over the edge. I lifted my hips off the bed and thrust my fingers deep into my snatch and uttered a deep, guttural moan.

"Fuck *me*," I said, feeling my pussy clamp down hard over my fingers as my body levitated a foot above of the mattress. I held my body in this arched position for many long seconds while the three of us grunted and screamed in simultaneous ecstasy.

Suddenly I remembered where we were, and how thin the walls were between the adjoining rooms.

I wonder if all the other guests are expecting a similar type of turndown service, I smiled, flopping down onto the mattress in exhaustion.

6

———

When the girls lay down on the bed after coming down from their tandem orgasm, I nestled in next to them, and we cuddled silently for a few minutes. It felt incredible to have two gorgeous angels lying next to me as we nibbled and caressed each other's bodies, with nobody wanting to acknowledge what had just happened. But as they became progressively more daring in exploring my body, Luna pulled away and peered at her friend.

"I think it's *Jade's* turn now to get a little direct attention, don't you think Gabby?"

Gabriella nodded, and Luna turned her head toward me, lifting the Rabbit vibrator off the bed.

"How can we put this thing to work for all *three* of us?" she said. "We have too many body parts for one device to stimulate us at the same time."

I raised myself up on one arm and pushed the vibrator back down onto the mattress.

"I think each of us have had plenty enough stimulation from that thing. I'd far rather play with some flesh and blood pretty *girls* than have another cock inside me."

"Mmm," Luna grinned. "What can we do for *you* now that you've given us so much pleasure?"

I peered at Luna's tubular breasts and smiled.

"I've been fantasizing all day about you fucking me with those pretty melons. I want you to diddle me with your special tits."

"Okay," she said, lifting an eyebrow. "But what about Gabby? It seems such a waste for her to just stand by and *watch*."

I peered over at Gabriella and hesitated as I contemplated how to get all three of us involved at the same time. Then a huge grin slowly spread over my face.

"I have an idea," I said. "I'll lie down on the bed while Gabby straddles my face, as you lift up my hips and support me from behind. That way, you both can get a bird's-eye view of the action while I get serviced from both sides."

Luna's eyes opened wide as saucers as she pictured the scene in her mind.

"Holy shit," she said. "That will be so hot. Plus, we can *both* play with your pretty pussy from that position!"

"What are you waiting for?" I said, lying down with my ass pointed toward the headboard. "Come here little girl and sit on my face."

Gabriella got up on her hands and knees and placed her legs on opposite sides of my head facing Luna. As she slowly lowered her dripping pussy onto my face, Luna raised my hips off the bed and pressed her chest into my lower back until my body was perpendicular to the mattress. Then she spread her knees for support and pushed my legs apart. As my feet dangled in the air beside her shoulders, she grabbed one of her tits and pointed her erect teat toward my quivering hole. When I felt her flesh press against my vulva, I grunted into Gabriella's pussy writhing over my face.

"*Uhhn*," I groaned, unable to speak with my mind spinning in pleasure.

When Luna began rubbing her breast up and down my slit, I could hear the soft sloshing sound my pussy made as my labia puckered in and out in involuntary reflex. Although I couldn't see what she was doing with Gabby's ass buried over my face, the thought of them both looking at my upturned pussy drove me wild with pleasure.

Just when I thought it couldn't get any better, Gabby leaned forward and encircled my inflamed bud with her lips, rolling her tongue over my gland while she squeezed my tits. With her head now getting in the way of Luna's titfucking, her friend lowered her face down my perineum and began licking my freshly washed pucker.

I couldn't believe that every part of my body was now being serviced by these two angels, and I grunted in mounting ecstasy as my hips began to shake from my approaching orgasm. When it finally hit me, I growled like a wild animal while Gabriella pressed her pussy hard against my face and moaned along with me as she sucked my inflamed bean like a lollypop. When I felt Luna's tits rubbing against the back of my hips, my juices spurted out of me like a geyser, spraying all over both of the girls' faces.

I came for the longest time as the two girls held my body in this upright position, quivering and spurting while the entire length of my perineum flexed in powerful contractions. I wondered if Luna noticed my rosebud clenching in powerful contractions from her front-row seat immediately above my elevated pelvis. Either way, the thought of my most intimate parts exposed to their direct view as I came mere inches away from both of their faces magnified my arousal as I grunted under the weight of Gabby's trembling hips. When I finally stopped cumming, Luna lowered my hips back down onto the mattress and both girls lay beside me, caressing my drenched tits and abdomen.

"Oh my God," I panted, watching stars floating above my head as my mind spun in a drunken stupor. "That was even hotter than I imagined. I don't think I've come that hard in my entire life."

"We *noticed*," Luna smiled, wiping my juices off her face with the back of her hand. "You really opened the taps unexpectedly on the two of us."

"Sorry. I do that when I'm especially turned on. And I've never been stimulated like that before. That was incredible."

"We enjoyed it just as much as you did," Gabriella said, sucking my nipples softly into her mouth.

"Really?" I said, holding her head gently against my chest. "I couldn't tell with your hips buried on top of my face. Did you cum too? I didn't want to leave you hanging–"

"Oh, I *came* alright. Maybe not with the same degree of fireworks that you did, but when you started squirting all over my face, you opened the taps for me too. I've never been in a threesome before. Thanks for inviting me into your room."

I peered over at Luna and smiled.

"I think we have your friend to thank for that. I'm guessing this isn't the first time the two of you have had girl-on-girl sex before."

"No," Gabriella blushed. "But never quite like this."

                               7
                     ____

"You know," I said, smiling at the two girls, realizing I had a once-in-a-lifetime opportunity. "We don't have a lot of time left before I have to leave town. We should make the best of our remaining time together."

"What else did you have in mind?" Luna said, propping herself up on an elbow.

"Everything we've done so far has been one-on-one, or just two girls enjoying each other's bodies. We still haven't had a chance for all *three* of us to come together yet."

Luna peered up at me and smiled.

"I have to confess that I was touching myself while I rubbed my breasts against your pussy," she said. "I came soon after I saw both of you climaxing."

"That makes me happy," I said, leaning in to kiss her moist lips. "But I was thinking of something even *more* interactive. Something where we all can be joined together at the same time."

The girls peered at me with a confused expression, shaking their heads.

"How is that even *possible*?" Gabriella said, pinching her eyebrows.

"With each of us having separate lady parts, how would we be able to touch them together simultaneously?"

"Surely you two have experimented with different types of *scissoring*?" I smiled.

"Yes..." Gabby blushed.

"Have you ever tried it *back-to-back*?" I said.

"How do you mean?" Luna said.

"I mean *ass-to-ass*. Two of us could rub our vulvas together, with the third one lying underneath as we ground our mounds together. I've never actually tried it, but I'm thinking it might work if we position ourselves the right way."

"I'm up for giving it a try," Luna smiled. "But who'll be on top and who'll be on the bottom?"

I looked at Luna and grinned.

"Something tells me you like to be the dominant one," I said. "Besides, I still haven't had quite enough of you. I've been dreaming about cunt-fucking you ever since I laid eyes on you. What do you say, Gabby? Would you like to have two sexy girls rubbing their pussies over top of you while you wrap your legs around our asses?"

"Oh my God," she gushed, turning her head toward Luna. "You weren't kidding when you told me about this crazy woman. I'm almost cumming just *thinking* about it!"

"It's *your* turn to lie down on the bed, girl," I instructed. "Would you like to take the inferior or superior position, Luna?"

Luna paused for a moment as she looked at me, trying to interpret my meaning. Then she nodded her head and smiled.

"I'll face her lower body, while you play with Gabby's tits. That way, I can watch her pussy twitching when we all come together."

"Works for me," I smiled, lifting my knee and placing my legs on opposite sides of Gabriella's hips.

Luna turned around and did the same thing, but with her head pointed toward Gabby's feet. We shifted our weight slightly backwards and when our asses touched, we arched our backs, angling our vulvas toward one another. When we felt our clits touch, each of us groaned.

"*Fuck*, yes," Luna hissed. "I want to feel you spray all over my ass when you come this time, Jade."

"My pleasure, hun," I said, peering into Gabby's eyes. "What do you say, Gab, are you ready to give this a try?"

"Damn *straight*," she said, pulling my head down and thrusting her tongue deep into my mouth.

As I swiveled my hips against Luna's ass and dripping pussy, I mashed my tits against Gabriella's chest, listening to her groan in my mouth. She tilted her hips and lifted her buttocks off the bed as I felt her grinding her mound against mine.

"That's it, baby," I purred. "Fuck my pussy while Luna tribs my ass. I'm going to spray all over your pretty cunny when I come."

"Mmm," Gabby moaned as I kissed her wildly.

The three of us were twisting our hips and grinding our pussies together, trying to find the right position where each of our clits received the ideal stimulation. I could feel Luna's labia intermingling with my own, and our pussies made nasty slurping noises as our asses smacked together. While our mutual passion escalated into a noisy cacophony of grunts and moans, Gabriella wrapped her arms and legs around my back and pressed her chest harder against my tits as she began to make funny squealing noises.

I knew she was close to cumming and as my *own* pleasure began to crest, I could feel it rushing toward me like a freight train. When the orgasm suddenly washed over me, the walls of my pussy suddenly clamped down hard and I began gushing all over Luna's bare ass and Gabby's pussy. Luna's buttocks began quaking next to mine as she howled in delight watching her girlfriend's vulva slapping open and shut in the throes of her own powerful climax. All three of us were climaxing now as we ground our pussies together in glorious union, grasping and clutching each other wildly. As we quivered, dripped, and squirted in mutual ecstasy for what seemed like an eternity, I suddenly became aware of how soaked the sheets had become.

It's going to be one hell of a clean-up operation for the next housekeeper,

I smiled. *But no matter—with the generous tip I plan to leave on my pillow when I check out, something tells me she won't mind.*

VOLUME FIVE

ELEVATOR SHAFT

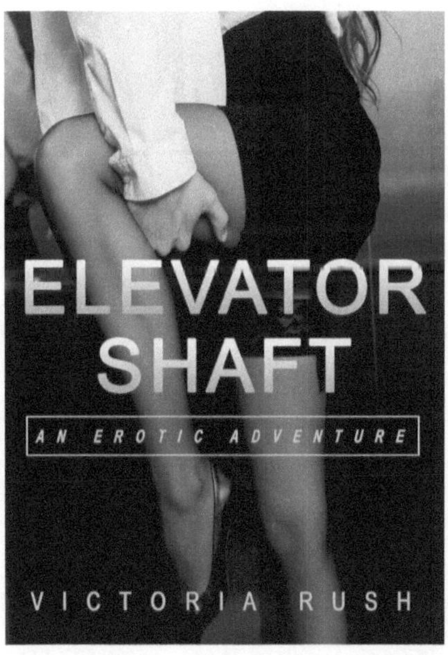

1

———————

I breathed a sigh of relief as I stepped into the elevator just after 5 p.m. on the day before Thanksgiving. My meeting with the creative director of Ogilvy & Mather Advertising had gone better than expected, and I felt elated at the prospect of working with the prestigious agency. We'd taken longer than anticipated to discuss the particulars of their Disney Studios campaign, but at the end of the day he'd awarded me exclusive rights to design all their new movie posters.

The view from their penthouse suite atop the Willis Tower was breathtaking. Chicago had been enjoying an unusually mild November, and I could see all the way across Lake Michigan on the clear autumn day. They'd feted me with a late luncheon in the Skydeck Restaurant on the 103rd floor and although I felt fully sated, I was looking forward to the annual feast with my family over the long weekend.

Ogilvy's offices had cleared out early in advance of the weekend crush, and I nodded toward the two lone elevator occupants as the door slid closed behind us. They were both dressed in expensive suits and looked to be about my age. The man standing to my right had thick ruffled hair, dark eyes, and broad shoulders that curved nicely in his tight wool suit.

But it was the woman standing on the other side of the elevator that caught my attention. Standing almost six feet tall in her Louboutin pumps, her perfectly manicured brows arched over aqua-marine-colored eyes and red pouty lips. Like the handsome hunk on the opposite side of the elevator, her busty figure left little to the imagination in her form-fitting skirt and blazer. My pussy twitched as I glanced downward, eyeing her long and shapely legs. Given how far they were standing apart and how hard they were working to avoid eye contact, I quickly surmised that they didn't know each other.

Funny how perfect strangers always find the quickest way to separate themselves in close quarters, I thought.

I glanced at the elevator console to confirm the ground floor button was selected, then I stepped to the back of the lift to get a closer look at the two passengers. They looked even sexier from behind, as I shamelessly ran my eyes over their figures. The man had a nice round bump lifting the back of his blazer, and I could make out the muscular curve of his thighs filling in his tight-fitting pants.

I bet that guy doesn't have much trouble getting his share of the action, I thought, suddenly feeling warm under my form-fitting suit.

But the woman's suit was even tighter, displaying every curve and valley of her sexy figure. As I stared at the globes of her firm ass clearly delineated in her snug skirt, my panties began to moisten thinking about how much I'd like to lick my way up her long legs all the way from her pretty feet to her steamy pussy.

Normally I tried to respect everyone's desire for privacy while traveling on elevators, but whether it was the after-effects of my three-martini lunch or my giddiness from landing the prestigious account, for some reason I felt the need to break the awkward silence in the lift.

I hope you guys have as good a reason as I did to work this late on Thanksgiving weekend," I said.

"Par for the course," the man said, turning his head halfway around and smiling half-heartedly in my direction. "Goes with the territory, unfortunately."

"Mmm," the lady grunted, staring impassively toward the front of the elevator. "No rest for the wicked in the urban jungle."

I peered back and forth between the two strangers, sensing some tension between them. Were they ex-lovers or disgruntled co-workers? Maybe they'd just been working late on a problem account and were exhausted after another long day at the office.

"Do you both work at Ogil–" I said, hoping to make some new introductions at the firm.

But as the pressure increased in my ears from the rapid descent of the elevator, suddenly the lights went out and the lift screeched to an abrupt halt.

"What the–" the woman said, breathing heavily.

"Oh my God!" I said, clutching my briefcase next to me as I quivered in the darkness. "What's going on?"

"It's probably just a power failure," the man said. "Everybody's been gearing up for the holidays and the little heat wave has been drawing a lot of power from the grid lately. I'm sure ComEd will have us back on track in no time."

"Are we safe, stuck so far off the ground?" I said nervously. "This is my worst nightmare – being stuck in an elevator suspended hundreds of feet in the air."

"Not to worry," the man reassured. "Modern elevators are equipped with multiple fail-safe mechanisms. An emergency brake automatically engages in the event of a power failure, so there's no way it can drop any further."

"What about the *cables*?" I asked, still petrified at the thought of losing control over the elevator. "Is there a chance they might fatigue or snap if this goes on for a while?"

"No way," he said. "There's more than one cable holding us up and each one is rated for much higher loads than our current weight. As strange as it may sound, this might be one of the safest places to be in the middle of a blackout. I hate to think how crazy it might be on the *streets* right now with all the traffic lights out."

"That's a small consolation," I said, beginning to breathe a little more normally. "I'd rather take my chances out there in broad daylight instead of being cooped up in this claustrophobic death trap."

In the pitch blackness, I could hear the sound of the woman's hands sliding frantically over the blacked-out console.

"What do we do now?" she said. "Can we communicate with somebody while we're locked up in here? I can't find the emergency call button in the dark–"

Suddenly, the screen of the man's cell phone illuminated and I saw his fingers tapping the surface. A flashlight lit up on the back side, and he pointed it toward the elevator control panel.

"This should help a bit," he said.

We could see a red button near the bottom of the console, and the woman slammed her palm against it repeatedly.

"Can anyone hear me?" she screamed. "We're stuck in an elevator near the top floor of the Willis Tower. Somebody help us, please!"

"The coms are probably down too," the man said calmly. "None of the electronic systems will be working as long as the power is down. I think we just need to wait it out until power is restored or the building's maintenance crew comes to retrieve us."

"Our phones," the woman said, turning her head in the direction of the man's glowing screen. "There are other ways we can call for help."

The two of us pulled our phones out of our purses and tapped 911. A message filled the screen indicating that the mobile network was temporarily unavailable.

"What the fuck?" the woman said. "The *phones* aren't working either?"

As the man lifted his phone to examine his screen, the backlight illuminated his handsome face.

"There's no bars. The power failure has probably disabled the cell towers too."

"Doesn't the phone company have back-up generators or something?" the woman said.

"Yes, but it will likely take some time for their systems to come online. But even if they do, every person in Chicago will likely be calling their family or emergency services to make sure everything is okay. I don't expect we'll be able to make any calls for at least a couple of hours."

"A couple of *hours*?!" the woman exclaimed. "How are we going to survive in this cramped elevator that long? What about air? Won't we run out of oxygen before then?"

"We're going to be fine, Elle," the man said. "There's plenty of ventilation ducts in the compartment, and with fifty floors above and below us, there's enough oxygen in the elevator shaft to support us for quite a long time."

So they do know each other, I smiled.

"You seem to know a lot about elevators for a guy wearing such an expensive suit," I said.

"Working on the hundred and fifth floor of the tallest building in the Midwest will do that to a guy. I'm a little claustrophobic too, so I did a little bit of research before I took this job. We'd *starve* to death long before any malfunction of the elevator would kill us."

"So we just stand here twiddling our thumbs while we wait for someone to come save us?" I said.

"It looks that way. But I'm guessing the emergency response people have their hands full dealing with a city full of panicked citizens. Plus, there's lots of other elevators in this building, so it's likely to be at least a few hours before anyone comes to our rescue. You might want to sit down and relax to make the wait a little more comfortable."

The man squatted toward the floor then leaned back against the wall and straightened his legs out in front of him. Recognizing that we might be in this for a long haul, I followed his cue and sat down kitty-corner to him against the back wall. Peering up at the woman, I saw that she was still tapping the surface of her phone, trying to make an outside connection.

"Why don't you make yourself more comfortable, Elle?" I said, trying to ease her distress. "My name's Jade. I didn't catch your name–"

"West," the man said. "The least we can do is try to get to know one another better while we're stuck in here. Make the best of an uncomfortable situation."

"It's either that or play Candy Crush on our phones until the power comes back on," I joked.

Elle exhaled a sigh of resignation as I watched her phone slide down the wall to my right while she plopped down on the floor.

"Why not?" she said. "I can't think of a better inmate to spend my time with while I'm locked up in here.".

"You two know one another then," I said. "Do you work together, or do you have some kind of *other* relationship?"

"Hardly," Elle huffed. "Not in a million years."

"We work together at Ogilvy," West said. "We handle two of the firm's largest accounts. I guess there's been a bit of a competition of sorts to see who would make partner first–"

"Not likely, with that lame-ass automotive account you've been handed. Can't you see that's a dying business with more and more people switching to foreign cars these days?"

"Maybe, but at least it's *reliable*. Not like that new tech account of yours–"

Suddenly, our conversation was interrupted with the sound of banging coming from inside the elevator shaft.

"What's that noise?" Elle said.

We paused to listen as the clanging sound grew louder and more frenetic.

"Could it be the maintenance technicians trying to open the doors above us?" I said.

"Unlikely," West said. "I can't imagine they'd be able to respond this fast. Most of them are probably stuck in traffic on their way home already."

"What is it then?" Elle asked. "Are the cables about to snap?"

The clanging noises suddenly changed to a rhythmic pattern of short and long taps.

"It sounds like an SOS signal. Probably from another group of people trapped in an elevator above or below us."

"That's not a bad idea," Elle said, pounding her fist against the wall beside her. "At least we know we've got some company."

"Not that it's likely to do us much good," West said. "There's not much either of us can do from our current locations."

Elle tilted her phone up, scanning the ceiling with her flashlight.

"If you're so clever Mr. Smartypants, maybe you can figure out how to get the lid off this thing and find a nearby exit?"

West chuckled softly in the darkness.

"There's a reason these things aren't designed to be evacuated from the inside," he said. "It takes a special key to open the lid from the outside. It wouldn't be safe for us to exit that way even if we could. Who knows when the elevator might start up again and pin us against the walls?"

"With all the time you spend in the gym," Elle huffed, "I would have thought you could jimmy up the cables to the nearest door."

"Yeah," West said. "I'm sure it's that simple. I'll get right on it."

It was obvious there was a lot more going on between these two than a competitive rivalry. Their little digs sounded more like a high school crush than a workplace disagreement.

"Is it getting hot in here, or is it just me?" I said, trying to break the tension.

I'd begun to perspire under my suit, and I was pretty sure it wasn't because I was afraid of plummeting to my death anymore.

"I feel it too," West said. "The air conditioning systems would have gone offline along with the power. And the radiant heat from outside the building is slowly creeping into the elevator shaft."

"Oh great," Elle said. "So now we're going to *boil* to death while we wait for help?"

"It shouldn't get much hotter than the temperature outside. I expect it will begin to cool as the sun goes down. You can always loosen your clothes to get more comfortable."

"That's the best pick-up line I've heard in a while," I chuckled.

"You have *no* idea," Elle sneered. "He's full of them."

"I guess it wouldn't hurt to take off my jacket and loosen my shirt," I said. "It's not like we can *see* anything in the pitch dark anyway, right?"

"I wouldn't put it past him to flash his phone you least expect it," Elle said. "We still have a few fleeting sources of power while we're waiting."

"Not for long," West said, peering at the glowing surface of his phone. "I'm already in the yellow zone for power. How about you guys?"

"I'm showing ten percent," I said.

"I'm down to *two* percent," Elle cursed. "I knew I should have replaced my battery during the last upgrade cycle. I can barely get through a full day at the best of times."

"We're consuming a lot of extra juice with our screens and flashlights on full strength," West said. "It's probably best to turn them off or at least switch to sleep mode to save them for when we really need them."

"Awesome," Elle said. "What do we do in the meantime?"

"Why don't we do what people used to do before the advent of modern technology and *talk* to one another," I said. "It sounds like you guys could use some more open lines of communication anyhow."

"What did you want to talk about?" she said sarcastically. "Our favorite hobbies and the unusual weather we've had lately?"

"Well it's probably best to steer clear of work," I suggested. "Tell us something personal about yourself, something nobody else would know. I mean, I'll probably never see you guys again once we get out of this predicament. Who else is gonna know?"

The compartment suddenly fell quiet as each of us pondered what to say.

"You know, it's strange," West said, breaking the silence. "I've always wondered what it would be like be in a situation like this. It's kind of *exciting* in a way, being left to our own devices without any outside stimulation."

"Kind of like being trapped on a deserted island," Elle chuckled.

"In a way, I guess. Makes you wonder what you'd do to pass the time, so far removed from modern conveniences."

"What do you think *you'd* do to amuse yourself on this deserted island, West?" I said, eager to steer the conversation in a different direction.

"Depends on who I was stranded with."

"What if it were just *you*?"

"I guess I'd have to scrape by on my memories. Or spend my time fantasizing about how to get off the island."

"And if you couldn't?" Elle said. "What would you fantasize about then?

"The usual macho stuff, I suppose. "That I was stranded in paradise with a supermodel–"

"Or two?" I joked.

"The more the merrier," West said.

"You men are always fantasizing about doing it with multiple women at the same time," Elle said.

"What about you then, Elle?" I asked, deflecting the attention away from West temporarily. "What would be *your* ultimate fantasy if you were stranded on a deserted island?"

"I'd probably go stir crazy all by myself after a while. I suppose I wouldn't be much different from West, dreaming about being stuck there with David Beckham or Brad Pitt..."

"Only *men*?" I said, fishing for more details.

"I dunno. I've never tried it with women before. But I suppose if we were stuck on a deserted island long enough, one thing might lead to another..."

"What about you, Jade?" West said, sensing a theme developing.

"I lean more toward women, myself. Although if I didn't have any other choice, I might be tempted to dabble a bit–"

"It *is* getting hot in here," West said as the sound of rustling clothes filled the compartment.

"Hotter than your deserted island fantasy?" I asked.

"It's getting there. All this talk about mixing it up with different partners is making me hot under the collar."

"Don't let us stop you from acting out your fantasy, West," Elle said. "It's just us girls in here. We won't tell if you don't."

"What exactly did you have in mind?" West asked.

"Something tells me you're getting uncomfortable in those heavy clothes for more than one reason," she said. "If you need to free the beast, don't let us stop you from getting your freak on."

"Um..." West paused, unsure if we were thinking the same thing.

"I think maybe West needs a little extra encouragement, Elle," I said. "Why don't you scooch up a little closer to me so he can exercise his fantasy more vividly?"

"This little adventure is getting more interesting by the moment," Elle purred, shimmying her hips across the floor to sit next to me. "I suppose there's more than *one* way to relieve the boredom when you're stuck in an elevator."

2

____

"So, West..." I said, hoping to capitalize on the rapidly developing heat in the room. "Tell us more about your little fantasy. Maybe it'll help keep our minds off this unpleasant situation we find ourselves in."

"Um, well," he said, happy to have a distraction to mask his real desires. "I guess I'd have to get to know these supermodels a bit better before we got down to business. I'd have to loosen them up a little before they thought about having sex with me, let alone with each other."

"Oh?" I said, playing along. "What would you want to know about us – I mean *them* – in order to get them in the mood?"

"I dunno, something about their families, I suppose. Maybe their relationship status. I'd need to make sure they were unattached before I proposed any kind of physical engagement. They might be kind of shy about wanting to try anything if they were already in a committed relationship."

"Let's pretend *we're* your fantasy supermodels for a moment," I said, nudging Elle's thigh playfully. "Let's see just how good your pick-up lines really are."

West shifted uncomfortably on the elevator floor and cleared his throat, imagining himself in a bar wedged between two women.

"Okay..." he said. "Well, first, of course, I'd ask them their names."

"I'm Jade," I purred.

"Elle," my partner-in-crime giggled.

"I'm West. Bit of a pickle we've gotten ourselves into. I suppose the first thing we need to do is make sure we have enough food and water to get us through this unfortunate turn of events. We don't know how long this situation might last."

"I've got a candy bar in my purse," I said, pretending to ruffle through my belongings.

"And I've got some bottled water," Elle said.

"That won't get us very far," West said. "But we might be able to catch some fish and create a pit to store fresh water when it rains. I guess our next order of business is to figure out how to send a signal to a passing ship so someone knows we're here. Do either of you carry a lighter?"

"I'm afraid I don't smoke," I said.

"Neither do I," Elle said.

"That's funny," West chuckled. "I always said that would be a deal-breaker whenever I met a pretty girl, but in this case we're going to have to find a workaround..."

"Are you saying you think we're *pretty*?" I teased.

"Well I don't want to swell your heads, but if I have to be stuck on this island for an extended period of time, I can't imagine two people I'd rather be with."

He's not bad, I whispered in Elle's ear.

He's got his moments, she nudged.

"So how are we going to let anyone know we're here then?" I said.

West rustled through his suit jacket and I heard a soft tinkling sound.

"I should be able to use my reading glasses as a magnifying lens to start a fire. Then we just need to find some fresh foliage or wet logs to create enough smoke..."

"You seem to know a lot about survival techniques for a guy who works in an office all day long," Elle huffed.

"Maybe I watch a little too much of that show Man vs. Wild."

"Well if you think you can get us out of this situation, we'd be willing to do just about anything you asked," she purred.

"Including eating bugs and drinking your own urine?"

"I'm pretty sure we can find something a little more palatable to eat between the three of us," I said, squeezing Elle's thigh.

"It's too bad we've gotten ourselves into this predicament so close to the holiday," West said. "You both must have been looking forward to enjoying a proper Thanksgiving meal with your families."

"I was just going to have an informal get-together with a few of my siblings at my mother's place," I said.

"What about you, Elle?" West said, fishing for more details about his colleague. "What did you have planned for the holidays?"

"I was on my way to the airport to visit my folks in LA when we got stuck in here. I hope they don't worry too much when they don't hear from me."

"Is there anyone *else* who'll be concerned about your whereabouts?"

Smooth, I nudged Elle. *He's looking to see if you're unattached.*

It was becoming increasingly obvious that West had more than just a working interest in her.

"Other than my *boss*, you mean?" Elle kidded. "Unfortunately, my job doesn't afford much free time for extra-curricular activities. What about you?" she said, turning back to West. "Who were *you* planning to spend some quality time with over the holidays?"

I smiled in the darkness, happy to hear the walls breaking down between the two co-workers.

"Other than my roommate and a few buddies on our house-league hockey team? We were just going to order a pizza and sit down to watch some football over the long weekend."

"You sound like a dyed-in-the-wool bachelor," Elle mused. "I didn't picture you sharing a flat with a buddy."

"Chicago's an expensive city for a single guy. Besides, sometimes it helps to have a wingman to navigate the social jungle. Speaking of living arrangements, it might be a good idea to start looking for a comfortable spot to spend the night–"

"We've already got plenty of shelter in our little corner under the palm trees," I kidded. I shifted my weight, feigning discomfort. "Although it *is* a little hard. I could use a pillow about now..."

West folded up his jacket and passed it toward me in the dark, and I placed it under Elle's knees, nodding appreciatively.

He's a gentleman too, I whispered, trying to encourage their reluctant courtship.

"So you're a *player*, then," she said, still unconvinced. "Where do you and your buddy bring your conquests when you want to have a little fun? Isn't it a bit cramped in your two-bedroom apartment? Or do you two create your own fun with each other?"

"Uh, *no*," West said. "I don't swing that way. What about you two? What are two pretty girls like you doing still single? I might say the same thing about you."

"Oh I like *men* alright," Elle said. "I just haven't found one yet worthy of my attention."

"What kind of man are you looking for?" West probed.

"The strong silent type, I suppose. Someone who knows how to treat a woman like a lady and is good with his hands..."

"Like someone who could get you out of a jam like this?"

"Possibly. But someone who's also a good lover and provider. He'd have to have a stable job and a good build..."

"Fair enough," West said, looking to bring me back into the fold. "How about you Jade? What are you looking for in a potential partner?"

"Someone with long slender legs who can wrap herself around my hips while I fuck her madly–"

"Jesus," West said, adjusting his equipment in the dark. "I've always wondered how you women do that exactly. How you make love without a–"

"*Penis*? Don't tell me you haven't watched your fair share of girl-on-girl porn? We can do pretty much everything a man can do, just without all the mess."

"What about–*penetration*? Don't you ever miss that?"

"We have lots of ways to get that when we're in the mood. Between strap-on cocks, double-sided dildos and all the special sex toys on the market, we can find plenty of ways to stimulate ourselves on both the inside and the outside. In fact, I'm carrying one in my purse right now. You never know when you might feel the need..."

"Really?" West said, his voice taking on a new sense of urgency. "Where do you use it? Isn't it kind of noisy?"

"Not this one. A friend of mine introduced me to it recently. It's called the Osé, designed by a woman. It doesn't vibrate so much as *throb*. It's incredibly lifelike, with a long undulating wand and an opening at the base that provides stimulation remarkably similar to a tongue–"

"Holy shit!" Elle interrupted. "Can I see this thing? I've never heard of a woman's vibrator like that."

"Of course," I said, happy to see that see her rapidly warming up.

I opened my purse and handed her the soft silicone instrument. She ran her hands over the long finger-shaped extension, then pressed her hand into the little hole.

"How does it work exactly?" she said. "It's not shaped like any vibrator I've ever seen."

"Feel for a little notch near the bottom of the base. There's two modes, each of which is activated with a press of the button."

Elle ran her fingers over the base of the object in the dark, then I heard her gasp.

"My God," she said. "It's *moving*. Like a real finger!"

"Exactly," I nodded. "It's designed to simulate the movement and feel of a real person. The curvature of the wand is perfect for stimulating your G-spot. Press the button again and see what *else* it can do."

I heard another click and Elle's body suddenly lurched next to mine.

"What the *fuck*?!" she exclaimed. "That feels just like a–"

"Tongue?" I said. "You won't believe how lifelike it is until you try it for real. Why don't you see for yourself?"

"Right here?!"

"Why not?" I said. "We're all getting pretty worked up with all this talk of sex with different partners. Besides, it's not like any of us can see anything in the pitch dark. If ever there was a safe place to try something like this, this is the time."

"I don't know," Elle hesitated. "It is intriguing, but I hardly know you guys..."

"Come on," I said. "I know you want it. I can feel your hips squirming next to me. Why don't you just slip it under your skirt for a moment? I think you'll get the idea pretty quickly what it's capable of."

Elle paused for a moment, then slowly began to spread her thighs apart. I could feel her hand rustling between her legs, then she gasped.

"Right?" I said. "Not like anything you've ever tried before, is it?"

"No," she panted, spreading her thighs further apart. "It feels more like a–"

"Real person?"

"Mmm," she purred.

"It might not be quite as good as the real thing, but you'll never know until you feel it against your naked flesh. Why don't you take your clothes off? We can place West's jacket under your hips if you're worried about the dirty floor. You don't mind do you, West?"

"Definitely not," he said, unbuckling his belt.

"Maybe for just a few seconds," Elle said. "But no peeking."

"Our phones are turned off, remember? No one will have any idea what you're doing unless you tell us."

"Okay, but no comments from the peanut gallery while I try this thing out. I'm self-conscious enough without you guys taunting me in the dark..."

"Maybe if we *all* took off our clothes together, it would make everybody feel more comfortable. That way, we could each explore our own bodies to the extent we feel comfortable. What do you think, West?"

"Way ahead of you," he said, pulling his pants down across the floor.

"Just go slow as you explore the device's capabilities," I said to Elle. "We'll be enjoying ourselves along with you."

"That does sound pretty hot actually," she said. "I'm getting hornier by the moment."

I lifted my hips off the floor, then pulled my skirt down over my legs and placed it underneath me. Then I grabbed Elle's hand and pulled it over my bare thigh, inches from my steaming pussy.

"That makes two of us," I said.

"Damn, Jade," she said. "Your skin is so warm."

"That's not the *only* part of me that's warm right now," I said. "Go ahead, let yourself loose."

Elle paused for a second, then unzipped the back of her skirt and shimmied it down over her ankles. Then she lifted her hips and pulled her panties off her legs.

"There," I said. "Doesn't that feel better? Now give our little friend a try against your bare skin."

Elle paused with the vibrator poised inches from her twitching pussy.

"Do you prefer to use the finger or the tongue?" she hesitated.

"Both, depending on my mood. Why don't you start by letting the finger caress you around your opening?"

Elle turned her hand and positioned the Osé so the finger bent toward her in rhythmic motions.

"It feels–*strange*," she said. "Like I'm being touched by a robot."

"But a very *sexy* robot, yes? Just pretend it's Brad Pitt's or David Beckham's or someone *else's* finger caressing you..."

"Mmm," she sighed, tilting her head back against the wall of the elevator. "That does feel better."

"You might want to tease yourself for a while until you get fully warmed up. When you're ready, feel free to insert it inside to experience the full capability of the toy."

"Oh, I'm getting *warmed up* alright," she panted. "How about you guys?"

I spread my legs further apart and rested my thigh overtop Elle's as I began to circle my hand over my clit. With the two of us sitting so close together, she must have felt the movement of my arm against her side as I began to stimulate myself manually.

"I'm burning up inside," I panted as the sound of my fingers rubbing against my wet labia filled the compartment. "How are you doing over there, West?"

"I'm thoroughly enjoying this fantasy," he panted. "I haven't been this hard in ages."

"I'm guessing there's something *else* hard in this room," I said, flapping my thigh against Elle's. "Why don't you put that wand inside you so you can fantasize along with us?"

I could feel Elle's arms tense up for a moment as she held the tip of the undulating finger against her opening, then she groaned, sliding down the wall. As I listened to the sound of the long appendage slipping inside her dripping pussy, I slid the fingers of my right hand inside me at the same time.

"Uhnn," she groaned, pressing the device firmer against her vulva.

"Do you *still* need Brad Pitt on your deserted island?" I said.

"Not with this thing by my side," she purred. "This is better than any man. At least it knows the right places to caress."

"Feels heavenly, doesn't it?" I said, curling my fingers inside my own hole to rub the front side of my G-spot. "Have you turned the tongue on yet?"

"Not yet," Elle panted. "I'm just enjoying the feeling of being stroked inside right now."

"Mmm," I said, feeling my juices beginning to run down the crack of my ass. I was thrilled that Elle had loosened up enough to feel comfortable sharing what she was experiencing. "Take your time, baby. We've got all the time in the world."

"That's what worries me," she grunted. "That we might be stuck in this elevator all weekend."

"I'm sure we can find plenty of other ways to keep ourselves amused if it comes to that," I said. "But don't worry about any of that right now. Just pretend you're stranded in paradise with your ultimate lover. What would you like him to do next?"

"I'd like her to lick me," she slipped. "I mean *him*. I mean whoever."

I reached between Elle's slippery legs and tapped the button on the underside of her vibrator one more time. She pressed the device harder against her body and squealed with a guttural moan.

"Oh my God," she groaned. "That feels incredible. I feel it's tongue. It's so lifelike..."

"Yes, Elle," I purred. "Imagine it's your fantasy lover worshipping your body. You're so hot right now."

"Is this how you do it?" she said. "I mean when you're with other women? This doesn't feel like any *man* I've ever been with..."

"Like I said, the toy is designed by a woman to provide feminine stimulation in the most erotic manner. But you'll never know what it really feels like to make love to another woman until you try–"

"*Fuck*, Jade," Elle growled. "I want to feel you against my body. This feels so good."

"Yes, baby," I whispered, lifting my hand to her chin and turning her face to meet my lips. As we began to kiss passionately, I pulled my hand out of my pussy and slipped it under her blouse, cupping her breasts and pinching her erect nipples. "Imagine it's *me* licking your clit right now."

"*Oh fuck, oh fuck*," she gasped. "I can feel it coming..."

"Yes," I purred, rolling my tongue around the inside of her mouth. "Come inside my mouth, Elle. I want to feel you twitching as I suck your button."

"Oh God!" she wailed. "I cumming, Jade! I cumming so hard. Suck my pussy!"

As we face-fucked each other imagining we were joined at the hips instead of the mouth, I heard West groan on the other side of the elevator as Elle began shaking uncontrollably against my body. Even though I hadn't touched her anywhere near her pussy, with our tongues intertwined and my hand squeezing her shaking tits, I felt incredibly connected to her. As she groaned into my mouth in the throes of a powerful climax, I suddenly gushed out of my opening, spraying my juices all over her bare legs while we quivered together in the darkness.

Something told me this was going to be just the start of our little fantasy adventure...

3

———

For the longest time after we came, nobody said anything, as awkward silence filled the compartment. All we could hear was the sound of quiet breathing while we all recovered from our powerful climaxes. There wasn't even any rustling of clothes while we lay there in the dark, completely naked. There was something incredibly erotic about knowing each of us sat inches away from each other, with our exposed genitals still throbbing in excitement.

After a few minutes, I heard Elle reach between her legs and pull the Osé out of her wet pussy with a distinct plop.

"Thanks for letting me share your little toy," she said, handing it to me in the darkness. "I'm sorry that I've made such a mess of it..."

"Mmm," I said, placing the tip of the wand in my mouth and sucking it loudly. "Don't give it a second thought. I like it that way. You taste exquisite. I only wish I could have felt you twitching in my mouth for real."

"With that vibrator's tongue doing its action between my legs and you kissing me at the same time, it was like you were actually there," she said. "I haven't been this turned on in a long time."

"What about you, West?" I said, trying to bring our silent partner into the loop. "Did you enjoy our little fantasy role play? Do you think your supermodels are getting sufficiently warmed up?"

"Damn near," he panted. "That was the most erotic thing I've ever heard. My only regret is that nobody was actually *touching* each other."

"Oh, there was plenty of touching going on, believe me," I said. "And from the sounds of things on the other side of the elevator, you seemed to be enjoying yourself plenty enough."

"Well, yes," he said. "But it's not quite the same as–"

"Having someone *else* touch you? What do you think, Elle? Are you ready to take it to the next level?"

"Maybe," she said, hesitating. "What did you have in mind?"

"Between the three of us, with so many different, um–*tools*–to work with, there's an almost infinite number of ways we can engage. We could pair up to start, then maybe swap partners before the three of us get together. What's your pleasure?"

Elle paused for a minute as she pondered the possibilities. I sensed the walls were beginning to break down between her and West, but there was also no denying her attraction to me.

"I've always wondered what it would be like to make love to another woman," she said. "With you being so much more experienced in that area, maybe you could teach me how to do it properly..."

I grinned at Elle's feeble attempt to mask her real desires. She had no idea what she was in for.

"I can work with that," I said. "How about you, West? Do you think you can hold on a little longer while Elle and I have a bit more fun?"

"Oh, I'll be *holding on*, alright. I'm hard as a rock again knowing I'm about to realize one of my ultimate fantasies."

"Well you go right ahead and enjoy yourself over there while Elle and I get to know each other a little better."

I turned to Elle and squeezed her hand gently.

"Do you want to be the top or the bottom?"

"What do you mean?" she said. "I thought that only applied to men–"

"When two women get together, usually one takes the submissive role while the other takes a more dominant role. It's the same with lesbians as with gay men."

"Okay..." she said. "I guess since I'm the neophyte here, I should assume the more submissive role–"

"Not necessarily," I said. "If you were to take a more active role, you could proceed at your own pace and explore things as they strike your fancy."

"I kind of like the sound of that. How should we position ourselves to start?"

I paused for a moment to think about the best way to give her optimal freedom of movement while still allowing me to touch her freely.

"Why don't you kneel overtop of me while I sit against the wall? That way we can kiss each other while we press our bodies together–"

"Yes," she said. "That sounds perfect. And it will be easier for you to tell me what to do next."

"Possibly. But something tells me you'll pretty soon figure out what to do entirely on your own. But first, take off the rest of your clothes so I can feel *all* of you up next to me."

"Mmm, yes," she purred. "I want to feel every square inch of your body next to me."

While the two of us peeled off our tops and shoes, I could hear West pulling his pants off his ankles and spreading his legs in a wide 'V' on the floor of the elevator. This time, he didn't want anything getting in the way of his enjoying himself while he imagined the two of us making love in the dark.

"Okay," I said, when I heard the last piece of clothing drop to the floor. "Come over here and sit on my lap. I want to feel your wet pussy rubbing up against me."

"Fuck, yes," she growled, swinging her legs over my hips and lowering herself on top of my thighs.

She leaned forward, pressing her tits against mine, and we locked lips as our tongues danced in each other's mouths.

"Mmm," she moaned, twisting her hips on my lap.

I could feel her mound rubbing against abdomen as a trickle of liquid ran down the front of my stomach. I lifted my hands and squeezed her tits, plunging my tongue deeper into her mouth. Elle wriggled her hips over the space between my thighs, trying vainly to get direct stimulation to her burning clit. I reached under her ass and slipped three fingers inside her pussy, and she began to hop up and down on me like a kangaroo.

"Yes, Jade," she panted. "Fuck me with your hand. I want to feel *every* part of you..."

As I listened to the sound of her sopping pussy ramming against my hand, I angled my wrist and pinched her clit between my other two fingers. She pressed her hips harder against my mound and I began to roll her hard button between my fingers.

"*Oh fuck*, Jade," she hissed. "That feels so good. Rub my clit while I fuck your fingers. You're going to make me come very soon..."

Although I wanted to stimulate myself while she rubbed her body against me, with my legs held closed by her vice-grip of my thighs, I decided to give all of my dedicated attention to her.

"Yes, Elle," I purred, slipping down the wall a few inches so I could suck on her tits while she writhed against my dripping hand. "Come for me, baby. I want to feel your pussy squeezing my fingers when you let it loose."

As I sucked on her hard teats, burying my face between her plump tits, Elle suddenly arched her body and wailed at the top of her lungs.

"I'm cumming, Jade!" she screamed. "Suck my tits while I cum all over your sweet pussy!'

The walls of her pussy tightened, contracting over my fingers, and much to my delight and surprise, she began squirting out of her hole all over my mound. With her juices suddenly spraying over my clit, I lurched my body forward as a powerful orgasm suddenly washed over me. While we mashed our tits together and sucked on each other's tongues, I heard West groaning on the other side of the elevator as he flapped his hand wildly against his raging hard-on.

Moments later, the sound of clanging metal began emanating from far beneath us in the elevator shaft. But this time, the banging didn't have any rhythm to it, sounding more like the noise revelers make when they celebrate a new year by thumping pots together. Apparently, our fellow captives had heard the sounds of ecstasy echoing through the shaft and were signaling their approval of our little distraction.

4

———————

Elle remained seated on my lap for many more minutes while we continued kissing and I caressed her wet labia with the tips of my fingers. It felt wonderful to have given her such a satisfying first lesbian experience, and I reveled in the feeling of her dripping pussy pressed against mine as our sweaty bodies rested against one another.

After a while, she pulled back a few inches and peered at me in the darkness.

"Thank you for making love to me so tenderly," she said. "I never imagined it could be this good. But what about you? This whole time you were focused on me. I want to touch you in the same places and make you feel as good as you did to me."

I smiled, running my fingers through her hair softly.

"I enjoyed that as much as you did Elle, don't you worry. When two women make love, it's more about the journey than the destination. We don't always have to get off to enjoy the experience of loving one another."

"I can see that," Elle said, lowering her head down the front of my chest. "But I've never felt a woman that way and I want this as much as you. Don't you want to feel my lips touching *you* now?"

I grabbed Elle's hair, holding her gently against my stomach.

"I do," I said, imagining her joined with me in a different way. "But not *that* way just yet. I want to feel your lips touching me in a different place."

"A different place?"

"I want to *fuck* you this time instead of making love to you. I want to feel your pussy rubbing against mine when we come together."

"Oh my God," Elle panted. "Yes, Jade. That sounds unbelievably sexy. What's the best way–"

I smiled as a devious thought crossed my mind. Up to this point, I'd felt a little guilty leaving West to his own devices, and I knew he and Elle were just waiting for an excuse to come closer together.

"I want you to get on all fours, facing away from me," I said. "I'll turn the other way around while we rub our asses together."

"But how–"

"Just trust me on this," I said. "I think you're going to like this. We won't just be rubbing our *asses* together."

"Oh," she said, quickly lifting herself off me and positioning herself a few feet away from me in West's direction.

I just hoped he hadn't spent himself entirely listening us making love the last time.

"How are you doing over there, West?" I said. "Do you think you can keep yourself amused a little longer while Elle and I try something a little different?"

"Knock yourselves out," he grinned. "I could do this all day and all night if necessary. I haven't been this hard for this long in ages."

"Don't lose that thought," I said. "We might be able to find some use for a *real* cock soon enough. Save a bit for us when the time comes."

"I'm not going anywhere," he said. "And neither is my dick."

I smiled as I positioned our clothes beneath the two of us, placing my hands and the balls of my feet on the floor, facing away from Elle. Then I shifted my weight backward until our cheeks touched.

"Mmm," Elle purred as she swiveled her buttocks playfully against mine. "I like the feel of your ass touching mine."

"That's not the *only* thing you're going to feel," I said, tilting my hips downward as my wet pussy caressed the inside of her thighs.

"Fuck, yes," Elle panted as she lifted her ass to press her vulva against mine. "This is so hot. I can feel your lips touching mine. Fuck me with your pussy. I want to feel you gushing against me again."

"Mmm," I said, mashing our cunts together. With our vulvas coated in slippery juices, as we slid our pussies against one another, a different kind of slopping sound filled the compartment.

"Fuck *me*..." West groaned, inches away from Elle's face with her body positioned near the base of his legs.

I could only imagine what was going through his mind as he listened to Elle and me fucking each other, and I smiled at how prescient his words were about to be.

Soon enough, West, I grinned.

As Elle and I gnashed our pussies together feeling our wet labia sliding over each other, I pressed myself harder against her clit, sliding her further in West's direction. Even though I was lost in the moment fucking her so hard, I had a second agenda for pushing her across the floor. I estimated that she was now only a few inches away from West's throbbing hard-on.

"Look between your legs, Elle," I said. "Even though we can't see each other in the dark, imagine you're watching our pussies rub together and seeing my tits shaking while I make love to you."

"Yes–" she said, then suddenly stopped, with our labia locked in a slippery kiss.

I sensed she'd felt something *else* in the darkness, and I knew her mind was racing about what to do next. But it didn't take long to begin hearing the sound of slurping noises coming from West's side of the elevator, as he began to groan excitedly.

"Oh God, Elle," he hissed. "That feels incredible. I've wanted you for so long..."

As he began thrusting his hips rhythmically into Elle's eager mouth, she hummed in pleasure while I resumed grinding against her pussy.

Knowing that the three of us were joined together in an erotic daisy chain ratcheted my passion to a higher level. As we all began to moan and whine in tandem, my body suddenly tensed up and I squirted hard between Elle's legs, spraying my juices all over her tits and her face impaled on West's pole. She groaned loudly with West's dick in her mouth, then I felt her buttocks spasming against mine as her body quivered in the throes of another powerful climax. At the same time, West began grunting in rhythmic sequence, jetting his cum deep inside Elle's mouth. The sound of the three of us moaning in mutual pleasure must have been music to the ears of the listening gallery a few floors beneath us, and I wondered if they might soon get the same idea that we had.

Suddenly I no longer cared if anyone came to our rescue for the next few hours. We were having way too much fun finding ways to pass the time on our own little fantasy island.

5

———————

For a few moments, we all remained still while we listened to the sound of the three of us panting in the darkness. This time there was no fanfare from others locked in the elevator shaft, now lost in their own distractions. Elle lifted herself off West's dripping cock and shuffled her body back over the floor, resting her back on the wall next to me. I reached out my hand and we interlocked our fingers, squeezing our hands together in acknowledgement of what had just happened.

Nobody wanted to say anything, embarrassed in the way lovers sometimes are the morning after an impassioned night of drunken partying. After all, we didn't really know each other very well, we were simply victims of the strange circumstance we'd found ourselves in.

It's funny the way a crisis brings people together, I thought.

I was about to break the silence when the sound of a distant voice suddenly perked our ears. As we lay still in the darkened elevator, the unmistakable sound of a woman moaning wafted into our chamber. But this time, the noise had a distinct cadence to it, like two bodies slamming up against a metal wall.

"Yes, yes!" the woman said. "Fuck me hard, Chase!"

I smiled, realizing we'd aroused the interest of more than our little group.

"It seems that we've started a chain reaction," West chuckled from the other side of the elevator.

"What else are people going do when they're locked up in close quarters for such a long period of time?" I said.

"It *is* kind of exciting," Elle mused. "Being stuck in the darkness, feeling our way around with a bunch of strangers..."

"I'd hardly say we qualify as *strangers* anymore," West said.

The woman's voice suddenly grew louder and more forceful.

"Oh God, Chase!" she hollered. "Pound my ass!"

"That's certainly *one* way to get to know each other better," I laughed.

"I can't believe I'm admitting this," Elle said. "But I'm actually getting turned on listening to all this sex in the darkness."

The woman's voice reached a crescendo as the banging noises echoed through the shaft.

"I'm coming baby!" she wailed. "Uhn! Uhn! Uhn!"

"Me too," I said. "What about you West? Do you think you have any ammunition left in your cartridge?"

I could hear the shuffling of clothes, as West reached for something to clean himself up with.

"I don't know what it is about this situation," he said, "but I haven't been this turned on since I was a teenager. It's like I'm thirteen years old again. My cock hasn't been this resilient in twenty years!"

"We shouldn't let all that energy go to waste," I said. "What do you think, Elle? Are you ready for some more fun and games?"

"I'm so horny, I could fuck a billy-goat right about now," she said.

I smiled, sensing the opportunity to bring the two colleagues closer together.

"I suspect you've got something a little better endowed on the other side of the elevator. I can feel the sexual energy between you two. If you don't fuck each other soon, there's liable to be a short-circuit in here before long."

"You're probably right," Elle said. "But what about you? What will you do to keep yourself distracted?"

"I'll let my fantasies wander for a little while," I said. I picked up the Osé vibrator resting on top of my skirt and slid it across the inside of Elle's thighs. "I've got my little friend here to keep me amused. You two go get yourselves better acquainted. I'll be just fine for a little while."

"Okay," she said. "But don't get too attached to that thing. I'm looking forward to tasting you with my *own* tongue when I'm finished with West."

"I'll be waiting patiently," I smiled. "Dreaming of all the ways we can pleasure one another."

"Mmm," she said. "Save that thought. I'll be back soon."

"Don't rush things too much," I said. "I'll be enjoying myself just as much as the two of you."

Elle kissed me sweetly on the lips, then skittered over to West's side of the elevator. Moments later, I heard the sound of wet lips kissing and two voices moaning. From the rustling sounds, I guessed that West had remained seated while Elle had assumed the superior position, sitting on his lap.

This time, she won't have to fish around for something to stimulate her pussy, I smirked in the darkness. As I imagined her sinking down over West's pole, I plunged the Osé vibrator into my pussy and began rocking my hips back and forth.

"Ohh," Elle moaned as the sound of rhythmic thumping emanated from the other side of the elevator.

"Elle," West panted. "I've wanted this for so long. You feel so good."

"I've been watching you for quite some time," she sighed. "I had no idea you were so well equipped."

"Uhnn," West groaned, slapping his balls against Elle's ass.

"Fuck me with your big dick, West," Elle grunted. "Let's give Jade something to think about."

"Oh, I'm *thinking* about it, alright," I said, tapping the button on the bottom of the Osé, activating it's tongue action. "I'm already fantasizing about what I want to do with the two of you when you're done over there."

"Do you want a piece of West's cock too?" Elle said.

"Maybe," I teased. "It depends on whether I'll have a pretty girl to play with at the same time."

"Mmm, yes," Elle said. "Do you think you might *like* that, West? Having your way with both of us at the same time?"

"*Fuck*, Elle," he panted. "I'm trying to keep it together. Don't make me pop off too soon. That's the last thing I need floating around the office when we get back to work. That I couldn't even last long enough to satisfy you–"

"Don't worry, West," Elle purred. "Your secret will be safe with me. Just imagine sliding your cock between our pussies while we rub our bodies together..."

"Oh God..." West groaned as his mind began to wander.

"Yes, baby," Elle said. "Come inside me as you imagine the two of us tribbing your big cock between our wet lips..."

I smiled at Elle's torment of poor West. But I sensed she was trying to excite someone *else* in the room, and it was working. As I squirmed against the pulsing wand and the slippery tongue caressing my pussy, I couldn't resist getting in on the action.

"Fuck, yes," I hissed. "I want to feel some *real* meat between my legs next time, Elle. I want to feel his pole trembling as he comes all over the two of us–"

"*Damn*," West groaned, as Elle pressed her ass down over his balls. "I can't stop it–"

"Yes, baby," Elle purred. "I feel you cumming inside me. Let it go while you dream about your fantasy supermodels. It's about to happen for real."

"Ohh!" I groaned, pressing the Osé toy harder against me as I began cumming in unison with West. "I feel it too. My cock is twitching inside me too. I'm cumming imagining it's *your* cock fucking me right now, West. Come with me, baby."

"*Uhnn, uhnn, uhnn*," West grunted, as Elle's pussy squeezed his pulsating dick.

By the time he finished moaning, I'd soaked the wet floor and clothes in front of me.

"Holy shit!" I sighed, sliding down the wall in contentment. "That was fucking hot! You two sure know how to drive a girl crazy."

"We're just getting started," Elle said, squeezing West's throbbing cock with the walls of her pussy. "I can feel that West is up for some more fun. It's time the three of us finally came together. Why don't you come over here and join us, Jade?"

"I thought you'd never ask," I said, sliding my body over to their side of the elevator.

I reached my hands out to find them in the dark and felt Elle's back as she sat straddled West's hips with his back against the elevator wall. I spread my knees over his legs and shimmied my body against them, pressing my breasts against Elle's sweaty back.

"Mmm," she purred. "You're so warm."

"And wet," West said, feeling my juices running over the top of his thighs.

"All the better to *fuck* you with," I said, reaching behind my ass to squeeze his balls. "Are you still hard? Because we're not done with you yet."

Elle turned her head to kiss me as she flexed her buttocks, gripping West's pole.

"Oh he's hard alright. But I want to get my hands on you before he gets any ideas. I've been dying to taste you since the moment I laid eyes on you."

"Really?" I said. "I thought you were just into men?"

"So did I until I saw you. There was something about the way you looked at us with that gleam in your eye. I knew I couldn't let you get away the moment the elevator doors closed."

"I guess the power failure happened at a fortuitous time then," I chuckled.

"It's the best thing that could have happened to us," West nodded.

I reached around Elle's back and squeezed her tits gently.

"So how do you want to do this? We better act fast before West loses that loving feeling."

"If you *really* want a piece of him," she said. "I suppose I can let you have first dibs–"

I smiled at Elle's offer, but I had other ideas for West's tool.

"I think we can find a way for him to get in on the action while we still have our way with each other."

"Really?" Elle said. "I'm not picturing it. How can we–"

"Never fear," I said. "I've had a bit more practice with these situations. Get back on the floor on all fours."

"But West has already–"

"Don't you worry about him. He's about to have the experience of his life. I'll lie underneath you in a sixty-nine position so we can lick each other at the same time."

"But I thought you said–" West protested.

"There's plenty in it for you *too*, West" I said. "Get behind Elle's ass and play with her from behind. That way, we can both have access to your boy parts."

Elle lifted herself off West's staff and positioned herself over top of our jumble of clothes. I slithered underneath her, grabbing the sides of her thighs, pulling my head between her splayed knees. West patted the floor with his hands trying to locate us and when he felt Elle's ass turned up in the air, he positioned himself behind her.

I reached up feeling for his dick and when I grasped his manhood, I gasped. It was bigger than I imagined, at least eight inches in length and six inches around. As I stroked my fingers toward its apex, I smiled when I felt his slippery head. He was still coated in Elle's juices and I plopped it into my mouth, savoring her delicious scent.

"Hmm," I hummed, swirling my tongue around his corona.

Elle could feel my breath blowing out of my nostrils toward her exposed pussy and she lowered herself toward my face, desperate to feel my touch. I pulled West's cock out of my mouth and rubbed the tip against her clit, licking his shaft from the base of his balls all the way to the tip, slathering my tongue over both of their glans.

"Oh God," West panted in delirious pleasure, feeling two women's bodies caressing his sensitive organ for the first time.

"Lick my clit, Jade," Elle growled, elated to feel my mouth against her sex finally. "Make West cum all over my pussy."

"I'd rather feel you come on my tongue," I cooed. "I've got other ideas for West."

I grabbed his shaft and angled the tip toward Elle's hole, and he eagerly sank his manhood into her tunnel. While they both groaned feeling my breath on their genitals, Elle spread her thighs further apart, lowering her vulva closer to my face. I pressed my hands outward against the inside of her knees until her flaming clit touched my lips. As I sucked her nub into my mouth and swirled my tongue over her shaft, she buckled under the weight.

"Oh my God, Jade," she hissed. "That feels incredible. Suck my clit while West fucks my pussy. I've never felt anything this good..."

As West rammed his cock in and out of Elle's hole, I felt his balls swinging against my forehead and I raised my hands to cup his sac, stroking the space in front of his anus.

"Fuckkk!" he squealed, hardly believing he was the lucky recipient of both our attention.

He leaned forward and grabbed Elle's tits from behind, pressing her face closer toward my steaming pussy. Smelling my box inches from her lips, she placed her head between my legs and began licking me like a puppy. As West began pounding her faster, I swung my arms around her hips and pulled her harder into my crotch. The thrusting motion accentuated the stimulation of my clit, as her tongue slapped back and forth against my inflamed nub.

"Mmm," I moaned, feeling Elle's clit growing harder in my mouth. "Suck my cunt, Elle. I want to feel you cum in my mouth as I squirt all over your face."

Elle nodded enthusiastically, trying to mimic the stimulation I was giving her on the other end. She was a quick study, and before long I felt my orgasm approaching as West's balls suddenly tightened and Elle began bucking wildly on top of my face. Within seconds, all three of us were wailing at the top of our lungs, signaling we'd reached the height of pleasure.

As Elle's clit began twitching in my mouth, I grabbed West's balls and squeezed them tightly while he tensed his buttocks and came inside Elle for the second time that day. I could feel his pelvic floor muscle contracting as he emptied his seed inside Elle's pussy, and the combination of sensations was too much for me to hold back. As Elle and West groaned in mutual climax, I tilted my hips and sprayed my juices all over Elle's face planted between my legs. We shook and grunted in unison for what seemed like a full minute before collapsing together on the floor in exhaustion.

But just as I was looking forward to a relaxing respite in the arms of my new friends, the elevator suddenly lurched and the lights came on as it began to descend.

"Holy shit!" Elle said, realizing we only had seconds before the doors opened and we'd be exposed to anyone waiting on the ground floor. "We better get ourselves put together before we're found out!"

We scrambled to put on our wet and wrinkly clothes, and as the elevator jerked to a stop, we looked at each other and smiled.

"That was one hell of a ride," Elle grinned.

As the elevator doors opened, we grabbed each other's hands and nonchalantly strode past the alarmed maintenance crew and rescue workers. The large wet spots and undeniable scent of sex on our clothes left little doubt what we'd been up to in the elevator. When we swung open the main exit doors and walked out onto the building courtyard, a large crowd was waiting to greet us. Without skipping a beat, they spontaneously erupted into a loud ovation.

I guess we weren't the only ones being entertained while we were locked up this whole time, I grinned.

Elle and West peered at one another, then leaned over and kissed each other passionately. I was happy to see that I'd been able to create more than one new connection among my friends at the Ogilvy & Mather Advertising Agency.

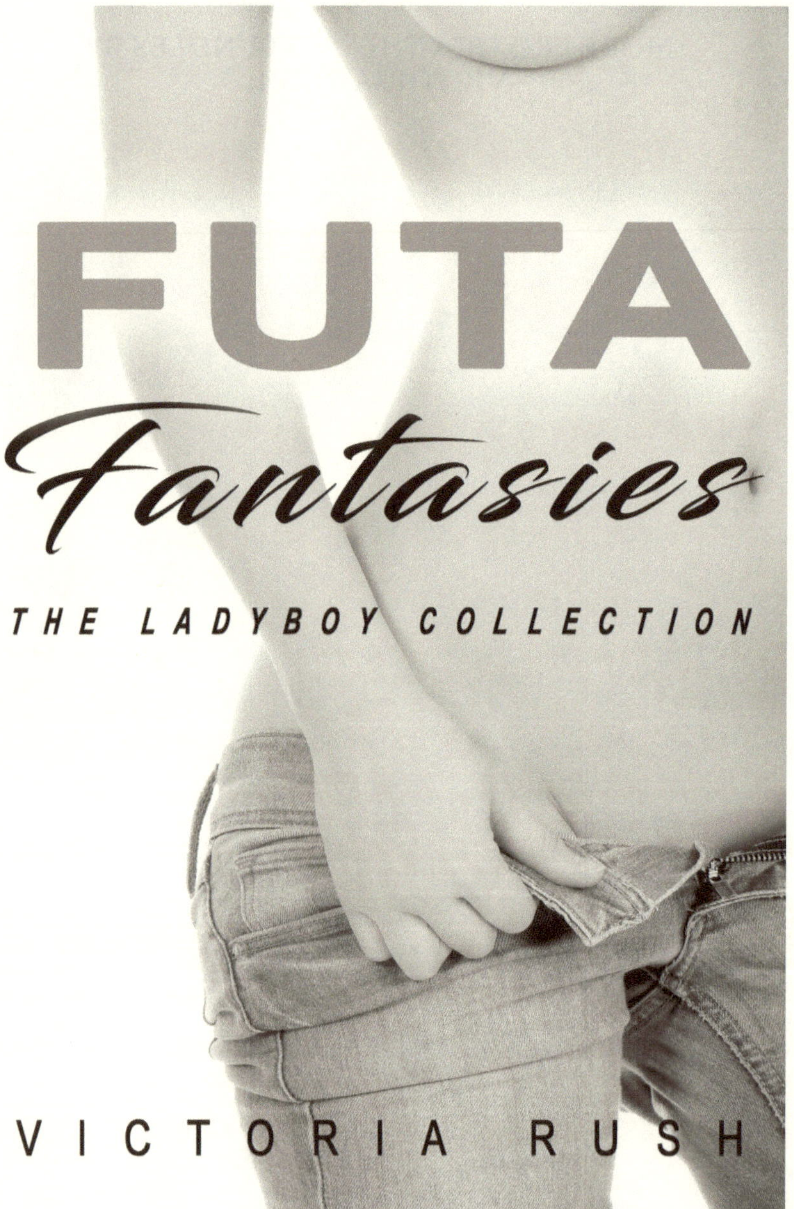

FUTA
Fantasies
THE LADYBOY COLLECTION
VICTORIA RUSH
Some girls have a little more to work with than others...